STO

ACPL ITEM
DISCARDED

SO-BWV-010

STRANGER NO MORE

Books by Iris Noble

Novels

ONE GOLDEN SUMMER

STRANGER NO MORE

Biographies

CLARENCE DARROW

THE COURAGE OF DR. LISTER

THE DOCTOR WHO DARED
  WILLIAM OSLER

GREAT LADY OF THE THEATRE
  SARAH BERNHARDT

JOSEPH PULITZER
  FRONT PAGE PIONEER

NELLIE BLY
  FIRST WOMAN REPORTER

WILLIAM SHAKESPEARE

STRANGER
NO MORE

by

Iris Noble

Julian Messner, Inc.
New York

Published by Julian Messner, Inc.
8 West 40 Street, New York 18

Published simultaneously in Canada
by The Copp Clark Publishing Co. Limited

© Copyright 1961 by Iris Noble

Printed in the United States of America

Library of Congress Catalog Card No. 61-13825

1163613

STRANGER NO MORE

1

The plane from New York had arrived ten minutes early in San Francisco.

"Ten minutes! There must have been a strong tail wind behind your plane," said the official of the Trans-Western Airlines to the girl in the green suit. "But don't worry about being early. Your aunt will find you. The only trouble is, Miss, you can't stand right in front of my counter; not when the passengers crowd up here."

Just at this moment there was no line-up of people waiting for him to check their tickets but there would be soon. He hated to ask this redheaded girl in the green suit to move, because she seemed so alone and because she looked so hopefully into the face of every older woman who passed; but she had been obstructing the traffic at his counter.

"I do hope she comes. The difficulty is that she may not recognize me; I had not considered that before." Katherine Norman gripped the handle of her overnight case a little more tightly. "My father received the letter from her before I embarked on the plane from Paris and there was a telegram awaiting me in the airport in New York. It said"—she pulled the crumpled yellow paper from her pocket—" 'Will meet you San Francisco airport 7:30 p.m. at Trans-Western Airlines. Aunt Debra.' So you see—"

"Yes, I see; but surely you know your aunt?"

"Oh, no. I have not been in the United States since I was a child," she answered.

He smiled. She sounded so grown-up, but he guessed she

could not be more than sixteen; seventeen, at the most. "You from Paris? I thought you didn't talk real American."

She looked at him, astonished. "What is wrong with how I speak? I am American. My father and I have always lived in Europe, but he is American and we spoke it together."

"I don't know; there's a little foreign accent now and then, and you don't use slang—" At that moment a stout man, loaded with baggage and waving his ticket, bustled up to the counter. The official looked meaningfully at her, so with a sigh Katherine moved away.

Now how was Aunt Debra to find her? She felt a sinking sensation in the pit of her stomach and it puzzled her. Was she afraid? She hadn't been, up till now, even though she had come alone all those thousands of miles. She had just been very excited. She was coming to America to live for at least a whole year and she had been looking forward to it so much. This peculiar sinking feeling bothered her. Perhaps if that ticket man hadn't thought she was a foreigner . . . if she knew what Aunt Debra looked like . . . if she could stand where Aunt Debra had told her to, instead of out here, where people moved and swirled all around her . . .

Then Katherine saw a sign to the right corridor, off the main lobby. The sign read RESTAURANT and she sighed with relief. She wasn't afraid; she was *hungry*—that was the peculiar sensation. At dinnertime on the plane she had been too fascinated, looking down through the window at the mountains and valleys the stewardess had told her were Nevada and then California, to eat her dinner.

She had nearly ten minutes. Perhaps the restaurant sold candy. She hurried, but at the door of the restaurant there were three girls, talking, and they blocked the door. She was forced to fall in behind them and she couldn't help overhearing what they were saying.

"So you'll be late for your date, Mary! So what? That Tommy

is a drip, anyway. Mom just put her foot down and we have to wait and meet these cousins. You can't duck out now."

Katherine had been tired, but she wasn't now. She was wide-awake and listening. These were American girls, girls her own age—the kind of girls she so much wanted to know. But they used such strange language. A date—now that was something she understood from the magazines she had read. A date was an appointment a girl had with a boy. But what was a drip? And why did their mother put her foot down? What did they mean by 'duck out'?

"Oh, all right," said the younger girl, moving slowly into the restaurant behind the others. "I'll wait. We'll go in and have a waffle and I can read this magazine—it's the new issue I've wanted. But don't ask me to lend you any money when I baby-sit next Sunday—not if you're going to call Tommy a drip. He may be short on brains, but he dances divinely." She caught sight of Katherine and smiled. "Are we in your way?"

Katherine smiled back, happily. Perhaps, in a few days, she would meet another girl like this at the American school and they would be friends. "No, not at all," she said.

The three girls vanished into the restaurant and Katherine followed, more slowly.

"I'm sorry; we don't sell candy," a waitress told her. "Wouldn't you like to sit down at a table and have a waffle? They are our specialty."

"What is it? I don't think I will have the time."

The waitress stared at her. "Haven't you ever had one?" She indicated the plate she was carrying and Katherine saw for the first time the crisp, brown waffle, with its strange criss-crossing and little hollow squares. It smelled wonderful.

Katherine's surprise delighted the waitress. "See over there? That's how they're made, honey." She pointed to a white-hatted chef who was visible behind a large window. Katherine watched while he poured in the batter and pressed down the top of the round waffle iron, quickly and firmly, so that a small spurt of steam escaped from under the edge.

It was interesting. She lost all sense of time. The chef scurried between coffee urns and great griddles where eggs and bacon were sizzling; he flipped pancakes high into the air so that they turned and fell gently onto their uncooked side. Katherine knew they were pancakes from Daddy's description: she had made Crêpes Suzettes for him once and he had explained that American pancakes were much the same, only bigger, and you ate them with butter and syrup. The chef pushed a filled plate of scrambled eggs and sausages out onto a shelf under the window and a waitress came up and took it from him.

A couple hurried into the restaurant and the man was speaking: "Sorry I was late, darling, but there was fog at the Burbank airport and we didn't take off until . . ."

Late. Katherine looked at the clock on the wall. It was nearly fifteen minutes to eight and she was supposed to meet Aunt Debra at seven-thirty!

With her heart hammering in her breast Katherine ran out of the restaurant and into the lobby, looking about her wildly. Why had she done such a thing? Daddy was used to her forgetfulness about time but Aunt Debra wasn't, and Katherine had wanted so much to make a good impression on this first meeting.

She saw a tall, thin figure of a woman standing over by the Trans-Western Airlines counter. There was no mistaking that figure, that face and that red hair. Aunt Debra looked so much like Daddy that Katherine's fear changed instantly to relief and happiness. Aunt Debra would probably scold a little, just the way Daddy did; but all the time there would be that great, hearty grin splitting his face, and his eyes would beam and he would hug her.

"Aunt Debra!" she called.

The woman turned. Katherine stopped running and her feet stumbled. The woman was undoubtedly her aunt; she had the same tall thinness that Daddy had, his same bony, prominent nose, the homely face and the red Norman hair, but there was no smile like his and her eyes were frosty. "Katherine?" A frown creased her forehead. "Didn't you get my wire? Didn't you know I'd be here at seven-thirty? I've been worrying, afraid I'd missed you or you hadn't come or hadn't received my wire. Where *have* you been?"

"Oh, Aunt Debra, I am sorry." She opened both arms wide to embrace her aunt, but the older woman moved to the side, slightly, so that she placed an arm around Katherine's shoulder, patted it a couple of times, and then drew away. Katherine's arms were left empty. One hand slid off Debra Norman's tightly corseted waist. "It was very wrong of me. I got in early and I was hungry, so I went to see if I could get a bar of chocolate," she finished awkwardly, despising herself for not telling the whole truth yet knowing instinctively that Aunt Debra would frown even more if she knew that her niece had been standing and watching a chef for twenty minutes.

Aunt Debra gave something that was halfway between a sigh and a snort. She smiled a tight, creased smile that hardly moved her lips, as if she wasn't much used to smiling. "Never mind that now. Welcome to San Francisco, Katherine, and to your new home. I'm glad you're safe and sound. Is that your small suitcase? Your other baggage is downstairs, then, waiting for us." Miss Noman led the way to the stairs. Her voice became a little more genial. "Well, Katherine, I would never have known you except for your hair. Luckily you've inherited your mother's looks: her blue eyes and fine skin and you don't have the horrible Norman nose." She rubbed her own ruefully. As she handed the baggage check to the porter she said, "Let me see—you were four years old the only time your father brought you to San Francisco for a visit."

"I'm afraid I don't remember it at all, Aunt Debra," Katherine said. "I do have a vague memory of a great, big round window, and Daddy says it was in your house."

"The bay window. Oh, yes. You were an extremely fat little

girl)—very determined—and you cried because you couldn't climb up into the window seat by yourself. I'm glad to see you've lost that fat and you're quite slim now."

When the porter carried her two suitcases out into the parking lot, Katherine remembered that her father had warned her that her allowance must cover all her personal needs and she must not expect her aunt to pay; so she dug into her purse for the tip.

Aunt Debra was shocked. "My dear girl," she protested when the porter walked away, "that was a dollar you gave him. Much too large a tip. We aren't rich people."

"I didn't know how much it was." Katherine got into the front seat next to her aunt and they drove off. "I always have a little trouble, just at first, getting money straight. I had to learn Italian lire and French francs and Greek drachmas—"

"True. I had forgotten that American money would be strange to you. I suppose there will be many things I take for granted that you will have to learn. It does seem odd that an American girl, seventeen years old, should know so little of America. I always thought it was nonsense for my brother to keep you abroad with him all these years, going to all those foreign countries. It's no proper bringing-up for a young girl." She spoke vigorously.

"But his work kept him there." Katherine protested faintly, not wanting to antagonize her aunt but feeling she must defend her father.

"His work! He could have got a job right here—oh, never mind, child. This is an old argument between Cyrus and me." She was silent, thinking her own thoughts, and so was Katherine.

Katherine's mother had died when she was too young to even remember her; all of her seventeen years had been spent, a solitary child, in the company of her father. She had roamed all over the world with him because Cyrus Norman's work was studying the folklore and legends of various countries. For this he went mainly to small, remote villages where old tales were handed down from peasant father to peasant son. He had never made much money. The little books he had written about his studies had brought in just enough income for them to be comfortable in a simple way.

Katherine had been happy with their life. Father and daughter were close and devoted to each other; they had kept house together in a slapdash manner and both had liked to experiment with odd cooking; they shared a liking for adventure and new places and people. But more and more as she grew up Katherine had begun to wonder what it was like to be an American. It was embarrassing when Italian or French girls asked her questions about her own country she couldn't answer. When her father had found her poring over magazines and books—anything which would tell her about life in the United States—he had announced, sadly, that it was time for her to go to her aunt in San Francisco, spend at least a year there, go to school and make American friends of her age.

Katherine was so absorbed in thinking of all this that she hardly heard when her aunt spoke again, and lost the first part of what she said.

". . . but it doesn't seem to have done you harm. You appear to be a mannerly girl. I must admit I was worried. You might have been all painted up with mascara and a lot of goo on your face or wearing your skirts above your knees. I didn't know what to expect and I might as well make it plain right now, Katherine, I'm not used to young people. You'll find I'm very set in my ways, I'm afraid; but if you understand rules and orderliness, we'll get along."

The vague unhappiness that Katherine had been feeling ever since she met her aunt became, suddenly, absolute desolation in her heart. Rules. Order. What rules? And what about Aunt Debra's love? Was she wrong in taking that for granted? She was glad it was dark in the car and that her face and brimming eyes could not be seen. It had never occurred to her that her aunt wouldn't be waiting affectionately for her niece, no matter whether that niece was tall, fat, with short skirts or long skirts, mascara or no mascara, and Katherine was shocked to realize that she had been on trial.

Maybe I still am, she thought, pressing her lips tight together to stop their trembling. I thought that if you were a part of a family—

"I work, you know," her aunt was saying, weaving her small car expertly through traffic. "I've been secretary to the general manager of the Marlborough Hotel for many years, so I won't be home until after five o'clock each day and I leave in the mornings about eight-thirty. There's a cleaning woman who comes in once a week to wax floors and wash windows, but we must do the rest between us and I expect you to keep your own room tidy. Never mind that now. We'll have time to go into it tomorrow. Tell me how your father is and how was your trip?"

In a subdued voice Katherine said, "Daddy sends you his love. He said to tell you he was well and he still has all his hair even though he has to wear glasses now—" Her voice wobbled.

Debra Norman gave her a sharp glance. "Child, you *are* tired." There was concern in her voice, if no kindness.

The minute they reached the house Katherine was bundled straightway into bed; a hot-water bottle was warming the sheets at her feet and Aunt Debra brought her a glass of milk and saw that she drank it before she snapped off the light. "Go to sleep. You're exhausted," she said as she left the room. There was only time for two small tears to slide down Katherine's cheeks before she was fast asleep—her first night in an American home.

Katherine woke the next morning wondering where on earth she was. The big, old-fashioned square room with its heavy furniture was unfamiliar; then she remembered. This was Aunt Debra's house and this was to be her own bedroom for a whole year. At first the memory of last night was a shocking and unpleasant weight; but when she saw the sun shining gloriously into her room, her spirits rose buoyantly to meet the challenge of the day.

It was early, so she tiptoed quietly to the window and looked out. The Norman house was on a hill and the houses across the street were lower; over their tops and roofs Katherine could catch a tiny glimpse of blue water and the graceful, soaring spires of a bridge.

She took a deep breath. She was *here*, at last! As for last night—well, she had been tired and probably had misunderstood her aunt. What could she expect of Aunt Debra? she scolded herself. Naturally the older woman was a little standoffish at first; even Daddy had warned her that his spinster sister had "prickles."

"It's been twelve years, darling, since I last saw her," he had said, drawing quick puffs on his old pipe. "And that was just a quick visit. Been almost twenty years since I lived with her. She was the older, so naturally she bossed me a bit. Spoke her mind pretty freely, but sweet under the prickles. Very shy, as a girl."

Katherine dressed quickly and quietly. To find fresh underclothing she hauled her suitcase onto the bed, fished around on the top layers but then, not finding what she wanted, tossed things out until she came to the clean slip and stockings. Her sweater was at the very bottom of the suitcase and when she pulled it out a shower of scarves and belts cascaded along with it, settling on the bed and on the floor.

Downstairs she peeked into the front room and saw the big bay window. So that was the one she had remembered! She smiled, thinking about a four-year-old Katherine so small and fat she couldn't climb into that window seat. Back of the living room was the dark-paneled dining room and, finally, the big kitchen. She looked at it in amazement. It was just like the pictures in the magazines . . . so big and white. The refrigerator took her breath away. She had never seen such a large one before.

An idea came to her. She would get breakfast and surprise Aunt Debra.

Out of the refrigerator came eggs, bacon, butter and milk; she would scramble eggs for breakfast just the way her father liked them. Turning to put the eggs on the table, she saw the waffle iron. Katherine looked at it curiously. It was just like the one she had seen in the restaurant. Very well! She would make waffles instead. In orderly array on a shelf she found cookbooks and she searched in one until she found the recipe.

First, though, the coffee for Aunt Debra. While it was perking she mixed the batter and plugged in the cord for the waffle iron. She left it to heat and rummaged in drawers for silverware, found it and also a pretty yellow cloth and went into the dining room to set the table. From there she could see clear through the living room and even out the bay window to the street and across it to a small patch of lawn and another house facing theirs.

A boy about her own age was on that patch of lawn. He was holding a hose and sprinkling water on a tall fuchsia bush and laughing at the antics of a brown spaniel who kept dashing in and out of the spray of the hose.

They interested Katherine, but she suddenly remembered the waffle iron. It was hot, so she spooned in a lot of batter and closed it. She found the maple syrup on a shelf and poured it into a pretty blue pitcher. The pitcher, her own glass of milk, the butter, cream and sugar she put on a tray; peeled oranges and arranged them in a pretty pattern of sections on a plate, then carried it all back into the dining room.

Now the boy across the street was doing the strangest thing! He was lying flat on his stomach and his head had disappeared. Katherine put the tray down on the table and went into the living room to kneel on the window seat and observe this peculiar thing.

Not even to her father had she admitted that, curious as she was about American girls, she was even more curious about American boys.

This one's head—oh, so that was what he was doing! He was pulling the dog out of the basement window and the boy's head and shoulders had had to go in the window after him. Katherine couldn't hear him but she knew he was scolding the squirming animal affectionately. Was he a boy? Wouldn't you call him a man? He was about her own age and very tall. When he stood up and threw a stick for the dog to chase, she saw that he had hair as brown as his brown jacket and that he was thin and nice-looking.

She started guiltily as she heard her aunt's footsteps coming down the steps—though why should she feel guilty watching a neighbor boy?

"You are up early, Katherine." Debra Norman was dressed in a neat, black, masculine-type business suit. Her graying hair was pulled back tightly, each strand in place; she carried gloves and hat and placed them on a chair, ready for her departure. "I thought you would sleep late this morning. It's a good habit to keep: early rising. I like that." She saw the dining-room table. "Why, how thoughtful of you! Not that I ever use that yellow cloth—it was one of your grandmother's. It's too good for everyday. You've set the table too. I had no idea you were so handy and competent and— *What's burning?*"

They both turned and ran into the kitchen.

The waffle iron was smoking black clouds. Batter had run down all over its sides and onto the table. When Aunt Debra pried it open with a fork, what was to have been a waffle, inside, was a black, burned mess.

"Oh, I forgot it!" Katherine wailed. "I didn't know how long it would take to cook it—I wanted to surprise you. It was the first one I ever tried to make."

"After this," said Aunt Debra curtly and disgustedly, "don't try something unless you've been taught. Ugh, what a mess!" She scraped and wiped until the waffle iron was reasonably clean. "I'll finish that tonight. After this you had better let me do the cooking. We can't afford to waste good food and I dislike a lot of muss in my kitchen." With an apron around her waist to protect her, she was efficiently whipping eggs and milk in a bowl. Every movement she made was quick, to the point, without the slightest waste of time or energy.

Katherine protested. "But I have done lots of cooking. Daddy says my canelloni and raviolis are the best he ever tasted, and I learned how to make a French ragout and Beef Stroganoff and—"

"I don't care much for fancy dishes," Debra Norman stated flatly. The cleaning of the waffle iron had apparently upset her usual time schedule and she kept glancing, anxiously, at the clock. She handed Katherine the platter of scrambled eggs and led the way into the dining room, carrying the coffeepot. "Plain, simple cooking is better for you and takes no time. I don't believe in being a slave to my kitchen; I have my menus for every day in the week and they are all the simplest things to prepare. Tonight we'll have broiled chops. You can scrub three of those large potatoes and put them in the oven at five-thirty, in case I'm not home then."

The scrambled eggs might as well have been sawdust for all that Katherine could taste, in her unhappy frame of mind. She had failed to please her aunt with the very first thing she had tried.

When her aunt had finished eating she pushed aside her plate and slowly sipped her coffee. "It's important that we get off to a right start, Katherine," she said. "If we both do our best to keep to certain rules and do our share of the work and plan a routine, then there's no reason in the world why your coming here should upset my life or why I should interfere too much with yours. I realize that you will expect, later on, to have your friends here and that will mean a certain amount of noise in the house—but that will be quite all right as long as you let me know in advance. On the other hand I'm accustomed to watching a favorite television program on Monday evenings, so I would appreciate your not inviting anyone that night. I've pinned a work and study schedule on the inside of your closet door; it may not be entirely suitable; we can discuss it later." She got up briskly. A few seconds later, hatted and gloved, she paused in the doorway and looked at Katherine. "Are you all right? You look a little peaked."

"I'm quite all right, Tante Debra," said Katherine, not looking up.

"*Tante? Tante* Debra. What did you call me?"

"I meant 'aunt.' *Tante* is aunt in French."

Debra Norman snorted. "Plain 'aunt' will do, thank you. I wouldn't use those French words if I were you, Katherine. People will think you're trying to be too sophisticated."

The door closed behind her.

I wasn't trying to be anything, thought Katherine. The tears she had been holding back came in a flood and she put her elbows on the table, her face in her hands, and cried. 'There's no reason why your coming here should upset my life.' That was what Aunt Debra had said. She doesn't want me. I'm just a burden and a duty and a responsibility to her, Katherine sobbed to herself. All she wants of me is that I don't bother her.

She found her handkerchief and wiped her eyes. Crying like a baby, she scolded herself. Seventeen years old and crying like a baby. She got up slowly and wandered around, wondering what to do with herself. Would it be like this every day?

No, there would be school and friends. America couldn't be all just like Aunt Debra.

A whole year of this! A year in this chilly, dark, big house where the books looked as if they had never been taken out of their places on the bookshelves; where the fireplace had a neat arrangement of ferns in it instead of logs or coals or a bright fire; where everything was in its place and in order—except Katherine. How could she fit into it? How could she live side by side with a woman as alien to her as her aunt, with her proper ways?

Katherine had a quick, clear thought of what it would be like at home, in the cottage with her father in the village of Belarno. A morning like this with the sun pouring into the open cottage door and she and her father finishing breakfast— the breakfast *she* had cooked—and laughing over the cat, who was cuffing her greedy kittens away from the bowl of milk outside the door; watching down the path where tall, stout Maria was approaching with one of her nine children; idly talking over the day's plans. "While Maria does the laundry, Daddy, I think I'll go to the beach for a swim." He would nod, but remind her, "Be back at ten. Mr. Manders is coming to give you lessons, remember." Then off he would go through the gay disorder of the kitchen, with its pots of flowers on window sills, to the comfortable disorder of the room where he worked, and she would lazily, happily, gather up the breakfast dishes to wash.

There wasn't a flower in Aunt Debra's house, not even a potted plant. No cat or kittens, no talkative Maria with whom she could gossip in Italian about the doings in the village. This house was too quiet, too dark; it oppressed her.

She had finished cleaning the kitchen and was starting upstairs to her room when the telephone rang. It was Aunt Debra.

"We were so rushed at breakfast," she said, "that I didn't tell you how sorry I am to leave you alone on your first day." Her voice sounded very worried. "Will you be all right? Your trunks came last week; they're in the hall and you could unpack them. I wanted to take the day off, but it is impossible. The manager, Mr. Dale, is out of town; the head waiter in the hotel dining room is too temperamental to be left alone without supervision, and I have a monthly report to get out. We'll go sight-seeing Saturday, but today I guess you'd best just stay indoors."

"I'll be all right," Katherine assured her.

The sight of the two trunks—one, battered and old; the other, spanking new—made her feel angry. They didn't belong here, the poor things, any more than she did. She carried dresses into the bedroom, shaking them and putting some aside for pressing. The others she hung in the closet.

It was on the third trip, while she was shaking out and hanging up an embroidered blouse which Maria had made for her as a going-away present, that she saw the paper pinned to the inside of the door and the schedule neatly typed on it.

7:00 A.M.   Get up, shower, dress, make bed.
7:30 A.M.   Breakfast.
8:00 A.M.   Wash dishes, leave stacked in drainer. Dry silver-ware.
8:30 A.M.   Leave for school (school starts at 8:40 A.M.).
4:00 P.M.   Mondays, vacuum living-room rug. Tuesdays, vacuum dining room. Wednesdays, sweep porch.
4:30 P.M.   Homework.

Katherine read no further. A blazing anger had swept over her. She was seventeen years old. Did her aunt think she was a child to be told what to do every second of the day? Except for her father's work and her own studies, whether those studies were with a tutor or in the occasional schools she had attended, there had been no other routine to their days. If she had felt like cleaning the cottage, she did. If she wanted to walk or swim or read, she did. Her father had trusted her to study hard and she had, because she liked books and learning; but he had never said '4:30—homework'!

In the school she had once attended in Switzerland there had been discipline—too much of it, her father had protested, when he took her away after a year. Every hour had been work, study, work, study, and he had thought there was too much Latin, Greek, languages and science for a thirteen-year-old girl and had brought her back to take up her gypsy life with him.

Even that had been a *school*, Katherine thought as she sat

on the bed and stared up at the hated schedule. Who ever heard of making such a routine out of every moment of her home life—if life with Aunt Debra could be called being in a home. It's a wonder, she raged, that she doesn't give me three minutes to brush my teeth and one minute to comb my hair.

She looked around her, at the bedroom, with distaste. Tan walls, dark furniture, white bedspread, white tailored curtains at the window, white frill hanging limp around the dressing table. Everything was spotlessly clean and everything was serviceable—the desk in the corner, the gooseneck lamp, the empty bookcase. The only spot of color was a pale pink china tray on the dressing table and the brownish portrait, over the bookcase, of a woman in an old-fashioned plumed hat and big puffed sleeves and, around her throat, a black velvet band with a locket dangling.

The expression on the face of the woman in the portrait was somehow familiar, and Katherine did not like it.

She finished unpacking her clothes but left the rest of her things in the trunks. Then she went downstairs, got out the vacuum cleaner and, in a spiteful mood, vacuumed the entire living room, dining room and hall. *That* will upset her schedule, she thought. Now I'll have four o'clock Mondays and Tuesdays to myself, to do nothing if I want to.

After it was all over she wandered outside onto the small porch. A middle-aged man was coming down the street and she was sure, from his uniform and from the leather bag he carried, that he was a postman. Her heart beat fast. Perhaps there would be a letter from her father—perhaps even a letter saying 'If you don't like it, darling, come right back to me.'

The young man she had watched earlier that morning came out of his house, banging the door behind him, and ran down the steps. "Hello, Beanie!" he called to the postman. "Anything for the Macdonalds?" He hurried across the street.

They met on the sidewalk: Katherine, the postman and the young man.

"Now, why can't you wait, Bob, until I cross over to your side? It mixes me all up, giving them to you out of turn like that." Though he complained, he was sorting out the letters and handing some over to the young man as he spoke. "And who are you, young lady? Haven't seen you in my neighborhood before. I'm Mr. Bean."

"I'm Katherine Norman," she explained. "I shall be residing with Miss Debra Norman for a year."

"Oh, you'll be *residing*, will you?" His eyes twinkled. "Then I expect this nice fat letter is for you, from Paris, France. If you get any more foreign letters, young lady, how about keeping the stamps for me? I'd like them for my collection."

"You beat me to it, Beanie." Bob Macdonald had been frankly eying the French stamps on the letter. Now he looked up and smiled at Katherine and gave her a conspiratorial wink. "You'll save one or two for me, won't you? It isn't fair that Beanie should get them all; he has the first chance of spotting all the foreign mail along his route."

Katherine thought it very rude of him to call this middle-aged man by a nickname, but she liked the way he smiled. It made a little crease in his tanned cheek—a crease that might have been a dimple except that his face was too lean for that. His eyes were dark brown and they smiled when his mouth did.

Now he was flipping through his letters. "One for me, two for my mother—that looks like a bill to me. I'll bet my sister's been charging stuff on Mother's account at the stores again. Dad'll be sore."

The postman had moved on with a friendly wave of his hand and a chuckling "So you *reside* here, do you?" and Katherine felt awkward alone with this Bob Macdonald. One of the things she didn't know at all was how to behave with young men. Was it proper of her to be standing talking to a strange boy, without an introduction? Or was Mr. Bean's friendliness the same as an introduction? She turned to go back into the house.

"Don't go yet." He stopped her. He shoved the letters into

23

his pocket and zipped up the jacket. "If you're going to be living with Aunt Debra for a year, we might as well get to know each other. Are you going to Golden Gate High?"

"Yes." That was the name of the school her father had been corresponding with for months. "I start tomorrow."

"We all do. What class are you?"

"Class? . . . Oh, I see what you mean." Without any conscious thought about it they sauntered to the porch. She sat on the top step while he lounged against the railing. "I'm not quite sure but I think I am what you call a senior. My school records caused quite a bit of trouble, at first, and letters went back and forth, but the school authorities finally told my father I would be admitted."

"That's fine. I'm a senior, too. Are you a foreigner? Sometimes you act like one and talk like one, and sometimes you don't."

She explained and he nodded his head. "So that's why you sound, sometimes, as if you'd learned English out of a book. Beanie got a kick out of your saying you 'reside' here instead of you 'live' here."

"Should you call him by that name?" she asked doubtfully. "It isn't very respectful."

"Everybody calls him that." He came over and sat down on the step beside her and now she saw that his thin nose was slightly crooked and, at the side parting of his hair, he had a cowlick so that a few strands stuck straight up. "He likes it. We're friends, he and I. When Troy, my sister, and I were seven years old he used to let us walk his rounds with him and we were the proudest kids in the whole neighborhood. We really thought we were helping him. And last Christmas he got me a job, as temporary worker, at the postoffice and I made enough to pay for my first semester's tuition at Stanford next year." He sighed. "If I make it."

She scoffed. "Everybody I know in Europe says American schools are too easy; that no one has to work hard."

24

He protested. "It's getting tougher all the time. You really have to study hard if you want to get into any college now. Colleges are jammed with applications and the best ones want only the top students. Senior year really counts. It wouldn't be as tough for me as it will be for you, because you're new to it all. But I'm hoping to be the editor of our school paper this year and that takes time."

"You don't have to be editor, do you? I don't understand what that has to do with *schooling*. Do the teachers make you work on the school newspaper?" Katherine crossed her arms over her knees and hugged them. She was delighted that this Bob was so easy to talk to, but she wasn't sure she understood what he was saying.

"Make you? Heck, no. Lots of students don't; like my sister, Troy, who thinks anyone who does any work he doesn't *have* to is crazy. She's nuts. She just goofs around all the time. Look, Katherine, someday I'm going to be a newspaperman, so any practice I can get now in school is all to the good."

"I still don't see what it has to do with school and how you can take ten or twelve subjects and still do those things."

"Ten or twelve! Holy cow, the most you can take are five majors and that's a lot, depending on the extra subjects you want." Now it was his turn to be astonished. "Did you take ten in schools in Europe?"

"I went to three different schools. The one in Switzerland was the most difficult. I had Latin and Latin conversation, Greek, rhetoric, botany, algebra, readings in French and English poets, two modern languages, French and Italian, and—"

"That's enough! My head's aching just thinking about it." He turned and looked at her squarely. "How come you got through all that without turning into an owl? You don't look like an owl. You look kind o' cute. You know, your eyes change color when you're thinking: they get darker when you're serious."

She had never heard anything so personal from a boy before,

and she blushed up to the roots of her hair. When he saw it he turned away and started whistling; then he changed the subject.

"How do you like San Francisco? Think you'll like living here?"

"I don't know. I haven't seen anything of the city except just this street and what little I could last night, when we drove in. Oh, I wish I could go roaming around! Always, when my father and I would go to a strange city, we'd just throw our baggage into a hotel room and then out we'd go exploring. In Rome we took a horse cab and we drove slowly about and he showed me all the famous things like the Colosseum and the Forum and the churches. He's talked to me about San Francisco so much that I just can't stand sitting here—and tomorrow I start school."

"What do you want to see most?"

"Oh, the cable cars! He tried to describe them but I still don't know what they are like," she said.

He stood up. "Well, come on, then. What are we waiting for? Put on a coat and I'll give you your first cable ride."

She hesitated. Aunt Debra had said not to go away from the house but, of course, Aunt Debra had thought she would be alone. "Do you really know my aunt? Does she know you?" she asked.

"Sure. I've known her all my life; I've lived across the street since I was born. We don't see much of her any more because she's busy, but when I was a kid she was good to us. It was always her house we came to first on Halloween for trick or treat."

"Trick or treat?"

While Bob explained, Katherine did some fast thinking—not so much thinking as impulsive deciding. Why shouldn't she go? Aunt Debra had sounded so very sorry that she should be left alone this first day and now she wasn't alone; she was with a boy her aunt had known all his life. Besides, she wanted to see the cable cars!

2

Half an hour later they were getting off a bus, in the midst of busy, downtown San Francisco. Katherine was pleased with it: there was a small green park squared on four sides by smart hotels and stores and office buildings. People walked by with a brisk purposefulness, as if they knew just where they were going and just what they'd be doing when they got there.

Clang-clang! She heard the sound and then she saw the small, painted cable car swaying up the street toward them, with trucks and motorcars dodging all around it.

Bob grabbed her hand. "Come on," he yelled. "We can make this one," and they sprinted out into the middle of the street and swung on board the little painted car that was just beginning its long, long climb up Powell Street. They sat outside. There was a small, boxlike affair at one end of the car where the passengers could sit, enclosed. But most San Franciscans seemed to like to sit outside, on long seats, facing in opposite directions out to the sidewalks, and in the middle, between them, the conductor hauled and pushed on a big stick that made the cable car start or stop. Every few moments he pulled on a bell.

Clang-clang! Clang-clang! They started to move. Katherine laughed with sheer exuberant pleasure. "It's like a little toy car sliding up a toy chain."

"That toy chain had better not break," Bob said, "or we'll all go sliding downhill. Having fun?"

"I love this. But I feel queer sitting out in the open like this and being carried along and all the people on the pavements looking at us and me looking at them." The wind tore at her short red curls and wound them all over her head. She had to keep one hand on her skirt to hold it down. She craned her head to look up at the conductor standing in back of her. "Do you drive this car, sir?"

"Nobody drives this car, Miss," he laughed. "We just go wherever that chain pulls us." They were rising to an intersection and he clanged the bell again and hauled the big stick back. People jumped off; more people jumped on. Bob got up and gave his seat to an elderly woman and he stood on the step facing Katherine, the step that almost brushed the pavement. Katherine half rose. "I want to stand up, too."

"Can't." He gently pushed her back. "Women aren't allowed to stand, only strong, brave men like me."

What fun this Bob Macdonald was! She looked up at him and said, "I don't see that that takes any strength— Oh, I see what you mean!" The tiny car had pulled its way up to the very top of the hill and had made a sharp, sudden, lurching swing around a curve and then around another, in the opposite direction. "You really do have to hang on tight, don't you? I don't think this vehicle is really safe." Her eyes were big and round, surprised.

Bob grinned at her. "Thousands of people ride them every single day. Have you ever lost a passenger?" he asked the conductor, and winked at him.

"Sure. All the time," the conductor winked back. "They drop off like flies. We have our worst trouble, though, with redheaded girls."

Katherine looked from one to the other. "I see. You are making fun of me. Please stop the car. I wish to get off."

"Oh, hoh! She's mad. And she's your problem, Buddy." The conductor looked at Bob.

There was space now on the seat and he squeezed in beside her. He lowered his voice and looked squarely into her eyes. "You aren't, are you? If you are going to be an American, you have to learn to take kidding."

She would have liked to be "mad," as he called it; but she couldn't stay that way. His brown eyes were twinkling and they were nice. A little twitch started at the corner of her mouth and then she broke out into honest laughter. "No, I'm not. I just didn't understand. I thought you were making fun of me and acting superior."

He shook his head. "I wouldn't do that to you."

They rode all the way down to the end of the line and Bob suggested that they walk to Fisherman's Wharf. It sounded exciting but Katherine said no. It was getting late. So they helped the conductor turn the little cable car around on its turntable, by both of them getting on one side and pushing. "We ride in it and we push it and we turn it around," said Katherine, enchanted. "I said it was like a toy and that's just what it is." When it was headed back into town again, they hopped on for another ride.

Once again on Powell Street, and before they took the bus back to their own homes, Bob did insist that she try a milk shake, when he found she had never had one. It was the final touch of enchantment to the day: she thought she had never tasted anything so good as that sweet, cold, thick, whipped-up milk and ice cream. "I shall have one of these every day," she announced.

"You do and you'll get as fat as a pig," he said.

Startled, she looked at him. American boys were certainly odd. One moment they said nice, flattering things and the next they could say you'd look like a pig. She had met a few European boys her age and slightly older; the studious type had no interest whatsoever in girls, and as for the other—she and her father had laughed about them. "I'm glad you don't fall for those romantic sighs and that hand kissing and the way they look at you and say '*Bella, bella!*' " Daddy used to say to her. No, she hadn't taken them seriously; but they certainly had always looked at her and talked to her as if she were the most feminine thing on earth. Bob's attitude was new. Half the time he seemed to treat her as if she were another boy.

She had just walked into the house, the clock in the hall was striking five, when Katherine saw the car stop at the curb and Debra Norman hurry up the steps. She was almost running, not at all like her usual self-contained self. She opened the door and called out sharply, "Katherine! Katherine, are you there?"

"Yes, of course. Here I am, Aunt Debra."

The older woman sank into a chair, holding her hand over her heart as she gasped for breath. "I was frightened! How could you have given me such a shock? Why didn't you answer the telephone? I called about three o'clock and then again at three-thirty and at four—I couldn't imagine what had happened to you. Where were you? I rushed home from the office, leaving half my work undone."

"I went for a cable-car ride with Bob Macdonald, from across the street. He said you knew him and I was sure it would be all right."

"But why," her aunt insisted, the Norman temper flaring up in her face, "didn't you telephone me? I think it was most thoughtless of you. You might have known I'd be worried."

"No, I didn't think you would worry." Katherine slowly took off her own coat and let it dangle from her arm; then she dumped it on the table. "I guess I'm not used to—well, not being trusted. Daddy always said I had common sense and he expected me to use it. And I'm not used to telephones. We've only had one a couple of times, when we were staying for short periods in big cities." Yet her own explanation lacked force, even to herself. She felt outraged at not being trusted; she felt ashamed of being thoughtless.

"Well, I was imagining all sorts of terrible things had happened to you. I must say this in very plain language to you: you're in my care and you are my responsibility now. What you and your father did was one thing; what you do in my house is quite another. It's not an easy thing for me to assume the

30

responsibility of a girl in my house, for the first time, at my age; I'm not used to it." Miss Norman got up and handed Katherine's coat to her. "Please hang this up in the coat closet right there; you'll find plenty of hangers. I want things to be as easy and pleasant as possible for both of us, and the only way it can be so is for both of us to abide by certain rules and regulations. I must know where you are at all times. On the other hand I shan't pry into your affairs; I shall respect a certain amount of privacy, just as I demand it for myself."

Katherine was hardly listening. She followed her aunt into the living room, but her own thoughts were pouring like rapids over the stones of her aunt's words.

This isn't a home where two people live together, she thought. This is a prison and Aunt Debra's my keeper. I owe her the very air I breathe; that's what she thinks. Rules. Regulations. Report where I go and what I do—

"I have to go back to the hotel as soon as I've had supper." Miss Norman slumped into a chair. If Katherine had been noticing she would have seen the lines of worry and fatigue around that determined mouth. "I don't suppose you scrubbed the potatoes, did you? Will you do it now and put them in the oven to bake? I'm going to take a hot bath before dinner."

When, at seven-thirty, her aunt had left the house to go back to work, Katherine was fiercely glad to be alone. Not that the house was pleasant. She walked around and it seemed to her there were scary echoes to her own footsteps.

She went upstairs almost on tiptoe and into her room. There on the dressing table, where she had put it before going out with Bob, was her father's letter. She picked it up and held it; just the touch of it seemed to take her right back to Italy and the cottage and her father and the sunlight and great, waddling, fat Maria.

At the thought of Maria she threw herself flat on the bed, on her back. How Maria used to rage against that husband of hers! She had a flow of such colorful language that sometimes Daddy used to caution her not to speak so freely in front of Katherine. However, Katherine remembered. What would Maria have said about Aunt Debra?

It was as if Maria were right in the room with her, hands on her hips, chin jutting out. "That old beetle!" That's what she'd say about Aunt Debra. "That sour old stick! That old maid! Better she should have got married, like I did; then she'd know what real misery is and have pity on others!"

Katherine rolled over and chuckled. This was very bad of her, thinking such things of Aunt Debra, but it really wasn't she who was thinking them—it was Maria. What would Bob say? That she was "kidding" herself?

She opened her father's letter and touched, lovingly, the familiar scrawl of his handwriting. She read and it was almost as though he were talking to her.

He missed her, of course. He had shopped that day in Paris for a warm, wool skirt to take back to Maria, and bought some presents for her nine children; he had wished that Katherine were there to pick them out for him. He had eaten in a good restaurant but the salad was not as good as she made for him.

She turned the page. "I know you'll be homesick and miss me at first, Katherine, but grit your teeth and hang on. I want so much for you to know your American heritage. I have tried to teach you to be an individual and think your own thoughts and judge your own behavior, but you are still young and you will make mistakes. If anything worries you, ask your Aunt Debra. It isn't going to be easy for you. You'll be given standards and values by your teachers, by your aunt and by your new friends your own age. They may not always agree. You'll have to select from among them what is best for you. Remember that Shakespeare wrote: "To thine own self be true, and it must follow as the night the day, thou canst not then be false to any man." It is the best advice I can offer you."

Katherine put down the letter. "To thine own self be true." What did that mean?

I don't know. Who am I? she wondered. I'm one kind of person with Daddy and I'm not quite such a nice person with Aunt Debra.

She wandered over to the dressing table and looked at herself critically in the mirror. Round chin, slightly rounded cheeks, straight nose, blue eyes—there was nothing special about them; nothing to make her any different from thousands of other girls. The one feature she really didn't like was her eyebrows. They were too straight. They didn't arch. The best feature was her skin, the creamy skin she had inherited from her mother.

There was nothing, she thought, that could be said for her red hair. It was short and it curled. In the frantic month before she had come to America she had given a lot of thought to that hair and tried wearing it in different ways. She had even, she remembered, giggling, gone to an expensive, fancy beauty shop in Rome. When her father had seen the result, he had put back his head and roared with laughter.

She didn't blame him. She had looked like an English sheep dog. So she had gone back to wearing it short and brushed up over her ears, the same as always.

Do I look young—too young—for seventeen? She tilted her head first to one side and then the other, and finally left the mirror no wiser than before.

I wish, she thought, I had a friend—a girl—who would tell me these things. Then I could see myself truly, reflected in her eyes. Daddy loves me too much, so that everything I do is right; Aunt Debra doesn't like me at all, so nothing I do is right. So I don't know what I am—and how can I be true to myself?

She looked around the room. This room certainly wasn't *her*. It didn't look as if it belonged to anyone; it had absolutely no personality.

On sudden impulse she went to her trunks out in the hall, on the second-floor landing. She must remember to call it the second floor; in Europe it would be the first floor, and the living room would be the ground floor.

Out of one trunk came her treasures. These were gifts her father had given her or little things she had bought herself and with which she couldn't bear to part. Out of it came the long, wide length of hand-woven blocked print of subtle greens and blues. She took it into the bedroom and threw it on the bed. What should she do with it?

Then she looked again and drew in her breath. It was beautiful just where it was, on the bed! She stripped off the white bedspread and used the print as a cover instead. It fitted almost perfectly.

Next out of the trunk came the blue and gold mosaic vase, so carefully wrapped up in a green flounced Grecian peasant skirt. Then the brown earthenware jug and plate. She tried the green flounced skirt against the dressing table and nodded her head. It would do. She cut it, measured it, cut it again, sewed it, until it made a handsome swirl around the dressing table. Then she took off the limp white muslin in scornful fingers and dumped it on the closet floor.

The vase on the top of the bookshelf; the earthen jug at the other end; in between, the plate so delicately colored. She burrowed down into the bottom of the trunk and brought up a picture of the island of Capri against the blue Mediterranean and spread it out flat, with heavy books on top of it. While she waited for it to straighten out, she unpacked more things: a pewter candlestick, a leather jewelry box with an oval inlay of white and green on top.

Last of all she climbed up on a chair and took down the picture of the old-fashioned lady, slipped it out from behind its glass frame and put the picture of Capri in its place.

Now the room glowed with color and life. She looked about her and slowly revolved, taking it all in, surveying it with intense pleasure. Here is where I'll live, she thought. Mr. Bean laughed at me but it is true: I *reside* with Aunt Debra. Here I live.

She was brushing her hair when she heard her aunt's abrupt

tap on the door. Katherine tensed herself. "Come in," she called.

Debra Norman looked around the room, astounded. "You have been busy, haven't you?" She rubbed her nose, then folded her arms. "It's a bit gaudy for my tastes, but it's your room. You can do as you please with it."

Katherine felt deflated, as if she had tensed herself for nothing. **1163613**

Her aunt continued. "I insist on privacy for myself and I shall see that you have it, too. If you want the room this way, that's your business." Then she noticed the picture of Capri. "Where is the other one?"

"I took it out most carefully. It came to no harm. It is there, on the desk," Katherine explained.

The older woman picked up the portrait and handled it as though it were precious. "I thought," stiffly, "that you might want it in here. It's the picture of your grandmother—my mother."

Katherine was aghast. "Oh! I didn't know."

"You might have asked," was all Miss Norman said as she left the room.

Now that the portrait was gone, Katherine wanted it back. She knew so little of her family and it would have been nice to have had Grandmother Norman in her own room. It was too late, now, because Aunt Debra was offended.

It seemed to her that everything she did offended her aunt. She cheered herself, just before she slipped into bed, by looking around at the gay, cheerful room. Such a difference colors made! The right combination of colors was so important—and, unbidden, there came to her mind that nice contrast Bob Macdonald's white sweater had made against his brown skin.

It was well to turn out the light if she was going to blush like that.

3

The next day was school.

"Golden Gate High School is north four blocks, turn right and over two more." Her aunt handed her a penciled map she had drawn. "Do you want me to go with you?"

"Accompany me? As if I were a *bambina*—a child?"

"We agree on something," Aunt Debra said drily. "I think you are old enough to handle this by yourself and it would be very difficult for me to take the time off from my work."

Katherine had given a lot of thought to the dress she would wear and finally settled on a blue serge jumper which was a copy of the uniform she had worn in the Switzerland school. She checked again to be sure she had fifty cents in her change purse and a sharpened pencil. Were her stocking seams straight? Why, of all days, did the soft bang on her forehead swirl stubbornly to the left side instead of the right, as it usually did?

She put on a good, poised front and said good-by to Aunt Debra very casually, but she was nervous when she opened the door and started out for school. The minute she saw who was waiting for her at the sidewalk, her heart gave a great bound of relief and delight.

"Bob Macdonald! Were you waiting for me?"

He grinned. "Why not? First day at school—you might get lost and wind up down at the water front. Come on." He guided her along at a fast walk. "We don't want to be late. I can't be. I promised I'd get there a little early and see the new faculty adviser for the school newspaper. We have to get started on the first week's issue right away, so I'll see him before I register."

He looked sideways at her, at the flushed color in her face. "Excited? Have you got everything you need?"

She showed him her pencil and he laughed.

"Tomorrow you'd better get one of these." He handed her the imitation-leather zippered case he was carrying. "They hold papers and notebooks and pens, pencils—everything. You can buy them at the store across from the school."

Katherine had been grateful he was escorting her; but as they neared the huge gray stone building and saw the dozens and dozens of other students on the street in front, she found she had a new feeling about Bob. It was pride in being with him. He seemed to know everyone, and everyone knew him. "Hya, Bob!" they called. "Hello, Mac," a few said. "How was your summer?" And one girl ran up to him and asked, "When is the *Bridge* coming out?"

Bob seemed to know what she meant. "In a week or so," he answered cheerfully. He turned to Katherine. "I have to leave you here. Sure you'll be all right? Just ask anyone and they'll tell you where you register and whom to see. I have to go around to the side door, first, and get this newspaper thing straightened out."

"I'll be fine," she said, and meant it. "It was very nice of you to think of me this morning."

"My pleasure," he smiled, and left her.

The warmth of his presence went with him. When he disappeared she was alone, feeling very much a stranger. She walked up the wide main entrance, which was set back from the street. It was crowded with young people, coming and going, chatting with one another, in twos and threes and in large groups. She felt as if everyone knew everyone and only Katherine Norman was a stranger, with all those unfriendly eyes on her as she walked up the steps.

The next hour was even worse. It was as if everyone spoke a language she didn't understand; everyone else knew just what he was doing and it was all a mystery to her; everyone was going in a purposeful direction while she was being battered back and forth with no idea at all of what she was doing. She had stopped the first person she saw and asked where she must go for admission. When she found that office, she was told to go to another office on another floor because hers would be a special case and could not be processed in the same way as the other students'.

For half an hour she sat on a chair in that office, watching through the open door the comings and goings of students. Never in her life had she felt so utterly lost, so completely lonely and strange. No one spoke to her. No one seemed to care what was happening or not happening to her. Wistfully she watched one group of girls just outside the office; they had cards in their hands; they understood just what those cards meant; she caught snatches of their conversation: "I'm taking Geometry IV. I couldn't get out of it." . . . "Poor you. Troy, can't you change and take English Lit with me at two o'clock?" . . . "Don't be silly. I'm not changing one single subject. I've got it all worked out the easiest way and everything will be a breeze for me."

The last speaker, the tall girl in the center of the group, seemed vaguely familiar to Katherine, yet she was sure she had never seen her before. But where had she seen a face like that, with that dimple in her cheek?

Just then a teacher came out of the inner office and approached her.

"Katherine Norman? I'm afraid we've had you waiting in the wrong place. I'm sorry. You're to take this card and go to Room 112 and ask for Mr. Johns. He will help you."

Her spirits lifted slightly. At least someone knew her name and where she was to go. At Room 112 she had to wait again, but this time it was mercifully brief and in five minutes the inner office door opened and a tall gray-haired man waved her inside.

"Did you have difficulty finding me, Katherine?" he asked,

smiling, settling down in a swivel chair behind his desk and waving her to another chair.

"Yes, sir. I didn't know where to go."

"You needn't call teachers 'sir' here, Katherine. Call me Mr. Johns. Well, the first days of registration and admission are always hectic and especially so for someone in your position." He picked up a sheaf of papers from his desk and looked at them briefly. "It wasn't easy to classify you, you know. We have the reports from the school in Paris and that helps us a great deal; still, your education has been quite different from ours. You are more proficient in languages than our students; you won't have to take the usual language requirements. You have studied Greek, which is not necessary here. You studied botany in Switzerland and that is fine. What do you know of American history?"

"The Constitution," she said promptly, and quoted the preamble. "My father always had a framed copy on his desk. And there are two houses of Parliament—I mean Congress: the Senate and the House of Representatives."

He smiled again. "Who was Patrick Henry?"

"I don't know, Mr. Johns."

"Abraham Lincoln?"

"Oh," eagerly, "I do know Lincoln. Every school child in Europe knows about Abraham Lincoln."

"Yes? What of his Secretary of State, Seward? What was called Seward's Folly? Is Hawaii a state of the Union? Who was Andrew Johnson? And Thomas Jefferson?"

At every question she had had to shake her head blankly. Mr. Johns's face became grave as he picked up a pencil, turning it over and over in his fingers as he thought out the problem. Then he picked up her schedule card and filled it in.

"English literature—required, but it will be easy for you. Civics VI. Gym you must take; physical education is a must. Advanced biology—that will be easy, too. And it's important you have some easy courses, because you will have to take both junior *and* senior American history. Miss Sunderman will give you special help and you will have to hand in papers and reports which the others won't; after all, they have been studying American history for years."

He handed her the filled-in card.

"Is that *all?*" she asked, looking at it. "Why, this just seems like nothing, Mr. Johns. At school in Switzerland—"

"Ah, I see." He linked his hands behind his head and leaned back in his chair. "Of course this isn't all, Katherine. I want to talk to you about your other interests. Do you want to join the Drama Club? Or Tri-Y or one of the other service groups? Are you interested in music or singing? We have A Capella and Madrigal societies."

She looked at him, not understanding. "That isn't school work, is it, Mr. Johns? I never heard of such things being considered part of schooling."

"Now we're getting into the basic disagreement between American and European schools, where they stress learning—facts, books, the cramming of knowledge into a student's head, as much knowledge as it will hold. American schools—well, I'll say *our school* since I'm not a spokesman for all of them—stress learning; but in addition we believe it is just as important that students work with one another to develop a rounded personality, learn self-government and what it means to be a part of society." He leaned forward and tapped a pencil on his desk. "I'm not saying we are right and they are wrong; certainly in the past we were too easy on students. Almost anyone could pass and almost anyone could get into a college. That's not true any more, but we still believe that these extracurricular activities are as important to your growth and learning as are books."

Katherine wasn't convinced. It must have shown on her face because he smiled and said, "Feel free to speak your mind, Katherine. You don't like the idea?"

She tried to say it carefully, so she wouldn't offend. "My father is sacrificing a lot to give me this year—and perhaps more years, in American colleges, if I prove myself. I wouldn't feel right spending his money, Mr. Johns, and my time in playing games and going to meetings and acting in shows. I don't think that's why I'm here. Oh, he wants me to have fun—but not *in* school."

He stood up, ending the interview and holding out her card. "Just the same, I'm not going to let you take any more courses. You'll have enough to do catching up on American history. If you hurry now, you'll just have time to see Miss Sunderman before lunch. And, Katherine"—as she turned to go—"I'll be very curious to see if you still have the same attitude by the end of the semester. Good luck. If you have any problems, don't hesitate to come and see me."

Miss Sunderman was a snappish, thin little woman with untidy gray hair. She was just about to leave her classroom when Katherine came in, introduced herself and explained her problem.

"Hmm. Well," jabbing a long hairpin futilely into a straggling wisp of hair, "you'll be a senior entering a junior class where all the juniors know more than you do. I don't know what Mr. Johns is thinking! It will mean a lot of special reading for you to catch up and I'll expect special reports handed in once or twice a week. Here is the book we are using, but I'm giving you another assignment right now." She scribbled on a piece of paper. "Go to the library and read up on the American Revolution; give me five hundred words by Thursday on the Boston Tea Party."

Katherine found the cafeteria down in the basement, but she was late and the room was full. Hesitatingly she went up to a girl standing last in line.

"Is this the queue? Am I in the right place?"

"Is this the *what?*" the girl asked her, astonished.

"She means the line-up," a boy in front drawled. "Queue is what they call it in England and places like that."

Suddenly all the lost feeling and the loneliness overwhelmed

Katherine. She was not going to wait her turn in line and then try to find a place at one of those crowded tables where it didn't look as if one extra chair could be jammed in. She fled back upstairs and out into the street. Down on the corner, diagonally across, she saw a sign FOOD SHOP and made her way there.

It was noisy, too, but mostly because of one large group at the long table in the back. In front was a small booth and it was empty. She squeezed into it, put her books down and took a deep sigh of relief. For half an hour or more she wouldn't have to cope with strange teachers, strange ideas and stranger students. Nobody was paying any attention to her and she was glad of that; after the waitress took her order, she was free to look around her and watch and listen.

That same girl—that same tall, thin, attractive, brown-haired girl with the dimple—was one of the most talkative of the noisy bunch in the back. It puzzled Katherine that she should seem so familiar. The tall girl was laughing and teasing a small blonde. "Flip, honestly you've put on at least five pounds this summer! Did you do nothing but eat?"

The blonde girl bobbed her head. "What else could I do? My dear parents insisted the whole family go to this ghastly camp up in the Sierras and, believe me, there wasn't a human soul my age for miles around. It was awful! I'd just eat cookies and wait for the mail and hope Pedro would write to me, but all he ever sent was postcards!"

A lanky boy grinned and pulled her hair. He must have been the Pedro she had mentioned because he said, "I hate writing letters. Besides, you only wrote once in four weeks."

A very good-looking young man, squarely built, compact, black-haired, sauntered into the restaurant, to be greeted by shouts from the back table. "Jet! Hi, Jet! Where've you been? We've saved a place for you!" He was in no hurry; he raised an arrogant hand in greeting and then nearly collided with the waitress who was bringing Katherine her sandwich. To side-step her, he bumped into the table and her glass of water tilted and nearly went over. Katherine and Jet reached it at the same time; their hands clutched it together.

"Sorry," he said. "I didn't mean to crash into you."

The water glass was safe and, in her relief, she smiled up at him. "It's all right. No harm was done."

The waitress tried to get around him, but he just stood there looking down at Katherine and then whistled softly. "Whoo-hoo! I haven't seen you around before, have I? I'd have known it if I had." Then he strolled on, leaving her with cheeks burning.

As she ate her sandwich she could not keep from observing the gay group at the other table. In her loneliness they symbolized everything that was out of her reach—a group that belonged together, knew one another, were easy and gay with one another. The one she didn't like was the arrogant, impudent Jet, and the one she liked best was the tall thin girl. What would it be like to be one of them—teasing the way they teased and laughing over jokes she couldn't even understand, talking about people she didn't know?

The restaurant was completely filled up by now, except for the booth seat opposite Katherine. In a few minutes a girl in a gray sweater and skirt asked if she might sit there. The two sat in silence for a while, then the gray-sweatered girl said, "My name is Marguerite Kelley. I saw you going into Mr. Johns's office today and you were in there a long time. Trouble with registration? I suppose that sounds nosy, but I was class secretary last year and I guess I got into the habit of noticing new students and worrying about them."

"It's nice of you to bother about me." Katherine told her of her difficulties in transferring to an American school and the extra work she would have to do learning history.

"That's too bad. If you have any time at all, I was wondering if you'd like to meet some of the other foreign students. I know you're American, but there are half a dozen kids from India and Japan and France here and they've formed a kind of informal International Group. Would you like to meet them?"

"Thank you—sometime, but not right now." Hurriedly Katherine tried to say no, but say it politely. The last thing she wanted was to meet foreign students; it was a group like the one at the big table—all Americans, the kind she had dreamed about—that she wanted to know.

For a while they were both busy eating. Thinking about this Marguerite Kelley, Katherine wondered why, when the girl was so genuinely nice and helpful and kind, she was not more likable. She hasn't any bounce, Katherine thought. She's so solemn and serious. Maybe, she rationalized, if she knew Marguerite better she would like her more; it was ungrateful not to appreciate the fact that someone had noticed her and thought about her.

She walked back to school with Marguerite and on the main steps they met Bob Macdonald.

"Hi, there!" he called. "How's it going, Katherine? I'm glad you two know each other. If there's anything you don't understand, just ask Marguerite. She's got all ten fingers in every pie in school. . . . Are you going on with the Drama Club this year?"

Marguerite's plain face took on a kind of gentle bloom and her eyes were shyly happy as she looked at Bob and said, "Stage manager, I think. I can't act worth a darn—I found that out last year."

The group from the big table in the restaurant swept by them, laughing and chattering. The tall thin girl was running up the steps, holding hands with a nice-looking, broad-shouldered young man, and, as she came abreast of Bob Macdonald, Katherine gasped, "Why, you're twins. She's your sister!" That was why the face had been so familiar; the girl was the very image of Bob except that her cheeks were slightly more rounded and she had the dimple while he had just the hint of one.

Troy Macdonald paused a moment, looked at Katherine and

then at her brother. "Sure, we're twins. Isn't it gruesome? Bob's the good twin and I'm the crazy one."

"Cut it out, Troy," Bob shot at her furiously. Even their voices were alike.

She was paying no attention. She was staring at Katherine. "I'll bet you are the one who's so mad about cable cars—Bob told me. You're living with Miss Norman? Well, we'll be seeing each other. Come on over and listen to my records sometime."

As the rest of them passed, Jet gave Katherine a bold glance. She distinctly heard the blonde Flip say to Troy, "Why do you want to bother with *her*? I'll bet she's as dull as Kelley."

Bob and Marguerite looked at each other and both made a grimace of disgust. "It's going to be worse than last year," he prophesied. "*The* Crowd, they call themselves. A bunch of jerks, thinking they are so important. All they ever do is play around, make fun of anyone who tries to study and see just how bad a time they can give the teachers. Not that I worry about the teachers—they can hold their own any time—but it's all so stupid. And Troy's as bad as any of them."

Marguerite sympathized with him. "They all dress alike, talk alike and then go around saying the rest of us are a bunch of sheep. Troy didn't use to be like that, did she, Bob?"

"It's so strange that you are twins and yet you are so different," Katherine said.

He nodded. "That's the whole point. When we were kids we were so close it was almost as though we knew just what the other was thinking. I'd start a sentence and Troy would finish it before the words were out of my mouth. We both got fed up with people saying how cute it was. When we hit high school, we just sort of flew apart and anything I did Troy was determined to do just the opposite. She was going to be herself, she kept saying. An individual, not half of a twin. I don't blame her but I sure wish she hadn't got mixed up with the Crowd."

He led the way into the school building. "Wait for me after your last class and I'll walk home—no, I can't. I forgot. There's a meeting today of all of us who worked on the *Golden Gate Bridge* last year. The newspaper," he explained when she looked baffled.

She was disappointed. Walking home with Bob would have made her feel so much less alone. That loneliness was worse in the afternoon as she floundered her way through the halls looking for her classrooms, trying to make sense out of instructions, assignments and beginning lectures from her teachers.

Until she reached her English literature class she had seen no one she knew, but in this class the alphabetical seating placed Katherine Norman just behind Troy Macdonald. Troy gave her a big grin before Miss Mailer rapped for order, and whispered over her shoulder, "This Mailer's the worst, the absolute, *living* worst."

"Your first assignment," Miss Mailer announced, "will be reading and memorizing John Keats's 'Ode to a Nightingale.' I shall read it aloud to you today so you may get the feeling and beauty of it, first."

She started to read and Katherine was stunned. Her own father had loved poetry, had read it aloud and she had loved to listen because he read so simply, so sincerely, never forcing an idea or a rhyme upon her. Miss Mailer's method was different. In a chip-choppy voice she hammered out each line, bearing down hard on those words or phrases which she evidently considered important for the class to notice. It was awful and Troy was right. Katherine squirmed in her seat as others were squirming, some sitting with their heads in their hands, bored, or, like Troy, paying no attention at all. Troy was busily scribbling something on a piece of paper.

Miss Mailer hammered on:

> "I *cannot* see what *flowers* are at my *feet*,
>   Nor what soft *incense* hangs upon the *boughs*."

Katherine felt indignant. No one should read who did it so badly; it was spoiling the whole poem, which had been one of

46

her father's favorites. Though she had met only three teachers so far, she had already been impressed by the qualities of each of them; even snappish Miss Sunderman was undoubtedly a good teacher. But this Miss Mailer—*tiens!*

She checked herself. Not even in her own thoughts must she use French or Italian. Aunt Debra had said that people would think she was trying to be sophisticated.

Troy held up the page she had been scribbling on, held it just high enough so that Katherine could see it over her shoulder. It was a drawing and a very clever one, a wicked caricature of an unhappy nightingale perched on Miss Mailer's head. It caught the likeness of the teacher perfectly, with her mouth wide open.

Katherine made a quick gesture of approval, her finger to her cheek.

Miss Mailer saw Katherine's gesture. She put down her book. There was a dead silence in the room. Slowly the teacher took the attendance sheet and ran her finger down the names until she came to one. She raised her head and said, "Katherine Norman? Will you explain what you did just now? I think you made a very rude gesture."

Without thinking, Katherine got to her feet and stood straight, hands at her sides, as she had been taught in Switzerland classrooms. "Oh, no, Miss Mailer, it was not rude." What had she done? She could not remember. Then it came to her in a flash. "What I did—it was the gesture of approval in Italy. Like this." She poked a stiff index finger into the center of her cheek and made a quick, corkscrew motion.

"I don't understand." The outrage had gone from Miss Mailer's voice but the stiffness remained. "I thought you were showing your dislike for the poem and this class. Please explain."

Katherine floundered. "It is, for the Italians, the gesture of approval. If an Italian does something very exceptional or sees something—how do you say?—excellent, he does this thing. I was told that it goes back a long time to when men had mustaches and twirled them when they were very pleased or wished to show approval. The mustaches have gone, so now the Italians have changed it to the finger twisting the cheek. It becomes so much a habit that I did not realize I was doing it." She demonstrated again.

The class laughed but they were not laughing *at* her; only as if she had done some amusing thing. Miss Mailer thawed and smiled.

"So you were expressing your appreciation of the poem and the reading," she said kindly. "I see. You may sit down, Katherine. It is never necessary to stand when you speak, in this school. I suppose they do that, too, in Italy?"

She was in good humor. Katherine slid back into her seat, feeling like a fraud. She had not meant approval of the poem or of Miss Mailer. She shrugged. If this silly teacher wished to think so, then there need be no mention of Troy's drawing.

Outside in the hall, after class, Troy was waiting. The blonde girl, Flip, was with her.

"This doll, Flip! This living doll," and Troy hugged Katherine. "She saved my life. If old Mailer had seen that drawing she would have had fits and I'd have been in plenty of trouble. Do that thing again with your cheek—show Flip. Isn't she cute? You should have heard her. She wasn't scared of old Mailer, not the least bit. Oh, I like you, Katherine Norman!"

It was fantastic that those last words should make Katherine feel like a top spinning around in happiness, but they did. This nice Troy Macdonald liked her and even that Flip was looking at her with interest. "I am very glad. Thank you," Katherine said. The bell rang then and they all separated, running for their next class.

4

The nice feeling that had come with Troy's praise lasted until after school and until she turned the key in the lock of Debra Norman's house. Its cold, dark, silent unfriendliness hit her the instant she walked in and its gloom settled down around her heart. She wandered listlessly, restlessly, throughout the rooms, not even taking her coat off. It had been such a confusing day and there was nothing here to relax or calm or reassure her. She was a stranger at school, a stranger here in this house and it gave her an unsettled feeling.

She tried sitting in the living room and turning to music on the radio, but she couldn't sit still. Something was nagging at her and she knew what it was: that schedule typed on the closet door. Finally she could ignore it no longer. She slipped off her coat, remembered to hang it up in the hall closet, got out the broom and dustpan, found an apron to tie around her waist and then went out and tackled the leaf-and-twig-littered porch with vigor.

The exercise helped. In ten minutes she was glowing with the warmth of her blood, and proud of how neat it all looked. Even the house seemed different when she came back in; she was alive and vibrant; she picked up her books and took them upstairs where the cheerful colors of bedspread and the mosaic vase and the picture of Capri suited her new mood. With the textbook she had been given in history class in front of her, she settled down at the desk to read about the American Revolution.

When she heard the key in the lock downstairs and her aunt's footsteps in the hall, she was still hard at work and enjoying it.

She had even written the first fifty words on the Boston Tea Party.

"How was school the first day?" Debra Norman asked with a weary sigh as she unwound a scarf from her neck and pulled off her hat. She looked tired. "Did you find your way around all right?"

There had been so much to tell, but now Katherine no longer had the desire to say it. How could she possibly understand, at her age? she thought. She helped hang up her aunt's coat, saying, "Oh, it was all right. I'll have to do some extra studying on American history. I don't know as much as the juniors do. Outside of that, it seems to be very easy."

"That's fine, then." No more questions. No more interest. "I think I'll take a warm bath and lie down for half an hour."

After dinner Katherine reluctantly put the Boston Tea Party aside for a while. It wasn't due for two days and she had to memorize that "Ode to a Nightingale" so Miss Mailer would have no reason to be angry with her. It wasn't difficult learning the lines which she had heard so often before. She was saying them over and over to herself when the telephone pealed downstairs.

"It's for you, Katherine," her aunt called.

Troy's voice hailed her. "What's the trouble? I can see your bedroom window from my bedroom window and you've been pacing up and down like a caged lion. What's up?"

"I was walking around while I was saying that ode to myself," Katherine explained. Excitement seemed to pour over the telephone lines with Troy's voice; Katherine was thrilled at being called.

"Well, come on over and say it to me; maybe I'll learn it, too. Maybe some of it will rub off on me and, if it doesn't, we can always play records or just talk."

"I'll be right over."

Aunt Debra was watching television in the darkened living room. She looked up when Katherine said she was going over to the Macdonalds', nodded her head, warned "Don't stay late, now" and then turned back to her television program.

By contrast the Macdonald house was full of light and color and noise. Mrs. Macdonald was a merry-faced, round dumpling of a woman and her husband was as tall and thin as his twins. Father and mother were sitting together at the round kitchen table when Troy took Katherine in to be introduced; Mrs. Macdonald was shelling peas and Mr. Macdonald was cracking walnuts across from her.

"This is the only place and time," he grumbled good-naturedly, "that I get a chance to see my wife and talk to her. Our youngest boy, David, chased me out of the study. He and two of his pals are making some kind of rocket missile in there. Bob's in the living room, and he says he's trying to write his first editorial and if anybody disturbs him his headline will be 'Murder Done at Macdonald Home.' You two *say* you're going to study?" He raised his eyebrows. "Just don't play those records too loudly, Theresa. I don't mind so much when they bellow; I hate them when they scream."

"Oh, Pop, can't you remember to call me 'Troy'?"

"Troy. What kind of nickname is that? A proper name for a Greek town but hardly for a girl."

Mrs. Macdonald snapped open a pea shell. "Get along with you two now and—mind!—do a little studying, too."

Troy's room was crowded. The one chair was piled with phonograph albums; a big square of tan matting over her desk was thumbtacked with snapshots. There were only a few books on the desk but there were stacks of records, a discarded sweater and an apple. Drawings by Troy were everywhere, pasted on her mirror, tacked onto the walls—clever, funny, witty drawings. Katherine looked closely at one or two and remarked, "But they are *very* good, Troy. Are you studying to be an artist?"

"Not me. I do those things for fun. Bob's always after me to draw some cartoons for his precious old *Bridge,* but that's too much like work. I only want to draw when I feel like it."

They settled down on the bed. "Now for the ode—"

Troy gasped. "Are you serious? I thought we were going to talk. Oh, all right. You say it and I'll say it after you."

They went through it once and then Troy said that was enough. "I have my own system. I get a general idea of the thing and then, just before I go into class, I say it over a few times, looking at the book. Enough sticks in my mind so I'll have a fifty-fifty chance of doing it right. At least, old Mailer will think I studied it and just don't have a good memory." She grinned impishly. "Now tell me about you. The whole Crowd noticed you in the Food Shop and old Jet went right out of his mind about you. He kept saying, 'Get that red hair and those dark blue eyes.' Man, he was really gone. But what are you doing in that orphanage-asylum jumper outfit you're wearing?"

Coming from Troy, there was no sting in the remark. Katherine looked down at her dress ruefully. "It isn't right, is it? I wasn't sure what to wear and this was the kind of uniform we had to have in school in Switzerland."

"Don't worry about it. Come Saturday, and Flip and I and Candy will take you down to our favorite shop and we'll really go to town on you. Do you have any money? An allowance? Good. Now tell me about Switzerland and all those places Bob says you've lived."

Troy was a good audience and Katherine felt warmed and happy talking about her life roaming the world with her father. However, she was as curious about Troy as Troy was about her and after a while she asked a question that had been puzzling her. "Why do all of you in the Crowd have such funny names —Jet and Candy and Flip?"

"Oh, those aren't our real names, any more than mine is Troy. It's really Theresa. Two years ago we all decided to change ours."

"But why?"

Troy shrugged. "I don't know. Someone started it." She pulled a large snapshot from the wall and held it so Katherine

could see. "That's me at the right and next to me is Chap—
we're going steady. Then comes Flip, you know her, and Pedro."
She described the others: the tiny, curly-headed Binky, who was
paired with Toby; Red and Candy. Red was called Red, she
explained, because he *didn't* have red hair and if it didn't make
sense it wasn't supposed to. Candy was snub-nosed, but aside
from that she had the haughty cheekbones and the slim, perfect
oval face of a magazine model. In the center of the picture,
standing a foot in front and alone, was the handsome Jet. In
this snapshot he was scowling.

"The rest of you seem to be in pairs. Who does Jet go steady
with?" Katherine found she was picking up the language that
Troy spoke, easily.

"Interested? Last year he went with a girl for a few months
but somehow she didn't fit in with the rest of us and he got
tired of her. Do you like him?"

Katherine said, slowly, "I don't know him. He is good-looking
but he made me angry today—he stared and whistled."

"Goof." Troy kidded her. "That's a big compliment from
our Jet. Candy's nuts about him but he can't see her at all, so
she and Red go steady."

"I thought going steady meant you liked someone very much
or even that you were in love with him. I don't know much
about it because I only read about it in American magazines."

Troy agreed. "That's the way it is with Chap and me and
Flip and Pedro but, you see, if Candy picks someone the Crowd
doesn't like she's out. We won't let in just anybody. So she has
to go with Red or nobody."

Katherine noticed that in the more recent snapshots all the
girls wore pretty much the same kind of clothes—full skirts,
blouses or sweaters. None of them, if they wore cardigans, put
their arms through the sleeves; they just wore them hanging
over their shoulders. In one picture all the girls wore strange
sticks in their hair. "That was the month, last year, when we
all went chopstick," Troy explained. "Flip came to school with

two of them sticking into the top of her pony tail, so then we all did it until the rest of the school caught on and imitated; then we quit."

The boys in the pictures wore loud sport shirts, then suede or corduroy jackets. They all had crew haircuts, but in recent pictures they wore their hair a bit longer.

Troy put a record on the machine and for a while they just lay on the bed and listened. It seemed awfully loud to Katherine and it wasn't long before feet pounded up the staircase and the door was slammed open.

"Pipe down, can't you?" Bob demanded. "I'm right underneath you, remember, and I'm trying to work."

"Work. Big stuff. Going to be the big, hot-shot editor, are you? I can just see you yelling at reporters, 'Get a scoop on that story, men; the presses are going to roll!' "

He reached over and yanked her by the feet so that she slid onto the floor, a laughing heap.

"I'll teach you to make fun of me," he said, keeping one hand on her head so that she couldn't get up and with the other, in a quick, deft motion, reaching over to turn off the phonograph. "I'll put a padlock on that thing so you can't play it. I'll smash all your records. I'll—I know what I'll do—" The grin that twisted his mouth was exactly like Troy's. "I'll tell Chap that Mother used to make you wear long woolen underwear down to your ankles when you were a kid and I have a picture of you to prove it!"

"Don't you dare!"

He backed out of the room. "You play that thing again tonight and see if I don't." Just before he closed the door he winked at Katherine and that wink made her feel wonderfully excited, as if they had a secret between them.

"You and your brother are so different, aren't you?" Katherine said. "You're so alike, physically; but you don't agree about many things, it seems to me."

"You are so right." Troy got up and smoothed down her hair

and her mussed-up skirt. "Look, honey, let me tell you some of the facts of life about school. If you're smart you'll learn how to study just enough to get by, without working yourself to death. Of course if you want to get in good with the teachers, then you have to play it their way; they love it when the school has the best football team and the best newspaper and puts on good plays. They and all the parents can congratulate themselves on what a fine school it is—but who's doing all the work? *You* are. They'll tell you how good this is for you, but don't get taken in by it; you're knocking yourself out and they're sitting back, taking the credit. You know what?" She put pillows behind her back and leaned against the headboard. "They keep on telling us these are the best years of our lives; that we'll look back on them as the 'carefree, happy days of our youth' "— Troy made a face—"and then they want to work us like slaves. Not for us; our Crowd isn't having any."

It sounded sensible, as Troy put it, yet Katherine wasn't sure. "I don't think I understand—"

"Honey, they'll organize every minute of your life if you give them the chance. Parents and teachers, they're all the same."

That was certainly true of Aunt Debra. Katherine nodded.

Troy went on. "It was Jet who figured it all out two years ago. Okay, he said, we still have to go to school and we're still living at home, but we're not kids any longer. We do the absolute minimum; we keep their rules when we have to, but beyond that we make up our own minds and our own rules and live our own lives. We're rebels," she said proudly. "And we stick together. They talk about loyalty to the school— phooey!—we're loyal to each other."

"That's exactly how I feel about Aunt Debra," said Katherine excitedly, "she doesn't really like me or want me. I'm just a duty to her. So I'll keep her rules, but my own private life is something she can't touch!" Resentment against Aunt Debra crystallized into a hard rebellion in her mind. She told Troy about the typed hourly schedule. "I feel just like a soldier doing sentry duty—hup, one, two, three—hup, one, two, three. About face, march!"

Troy laughed but she said, "How ghastly! Mom and Dad are different. For parents they're pretty okay. Still, even they are after me all the time: 'If Bob can do this, why can't you? Haven't you any ambition? Don't you want to make something of yourself?' What they really want is for me to be what *they* want me to be."

Katherine had a lot to think about as she crossed the street. It was dark and she was late; she was grateful for the porch light that Aunt Debra had left on for her. She was glad, too, that her aunt was already in her own bedroom with the door closed. "That you, Katherine?" came her sleepy voice, and Katherine had only to say "Yes, Aunt Debra" and slip into her own room.

Both Troy and Bob seem to like me, she thought as she undressed. I like both of them. Daddy would say they were two different kettles of fish, entirely, and I guess they are. Which one would he like best? That was easy; he'd choose Bob. But why, when Troy was so much fun, so gay, so lighthearted? Bob's too busy to be bothered with me, she thought as she snuggled under the covers and snapped off the bedside lamp, and Troy has already said she'd go with me Saturday to buy clothes . . .

She drifted off to sleep.

The next morning she told her aunt about the Saturday shopping expedition.

"I thought we—I thought you would want to drive around and see the city with me Saturday." Her aunt rubbed her nose, a habit Katherine noted. "Well, it doesn't really matter. We can go Sunday. I liked that dress you were wearing yesterday but I don't presume to know what's the style for young girls."

Katherine washed a dish and dipped it into the rinse water and then stuck it into the drainer. "Troy said I looked like something from an orphan asylum. It wasn't *right*, Aunt Debra. I hate to spend Daddy's money on clothes, but I do want to look like the other girls."

Debra Norman had been putting the orange juice and milk into the refrigerator. Now she straightened up, put her hands on her hips and regarded Katherine fiercely. "I don't care what it costs—if your allowance isn't enough, you come to me and I'll give you some—but you're going to be as well dressed as the other girls."

"Why, Aunt Debra!"

"I mean it. After my parents died and I was twenty and Cyrus, your father, was sixteen, we had very little money. I had to go to work. I didn't mind that but I did mind wearing old clothes, long after they had gone out of style. I know what it means when you're young and want pretty things!"

Now what, Katherine thought as she walked to school, can I make of that? Who would have thought of her aunt as ever being young, ever thinking of pretty clothes, ever minding what she looked like as long as she was neat and clean?

By eight-forty she was in her registry room where, for ten minutes before the students went to their regular classrooms, the teacher explained some changes in schedules, made several announcements and checked the attendance record. Those interested in Red Cross work were to see Mr. Allen. Mr. Johns would be coaching the Drama Club. Driving lessons would start in a week for those who could qualify as to age requirement and learner's permit.

Driving lessons! Katherine sniffed. These American schools were really ridiculous.

The first strangeness of the school had worn off; she did not have quite that lost feeling of yesterday. Marguerite Kelley passed her in the hall and said "See you for lunch in the cafeteria?" and Katherine nodded yes.

However, she didn't go. At eleven-fifteen as she started down the basement steps Troy Macdonald came up behind her and grabbed one arm and the blonde Flip took the other. "Come on," they urged. "We never eat in the cafeteria because you can't talk there and, half the time, there isn't a big enough table for our whole Crowd to sit together. We always go to the Food Shop."

We. She was one of them; they were taking it for granted that she belonged with them. It was a marvelous feeling, this belonging, and Katherine let herself joyfully be swept along with them. Outside, Chap and Pedro and Binky were waiting and they sauntered over to the Food Shop in a group.

The small restaurant was crowded. Every stool was taken at the counter as well as all the small booths, but no one had ventured to take a place at the big one, where Candy and Red were sitting and waiting. It was their special booth. The proprietor, a little, worried, bald man, seemed to acknowledge it was theirs. He looked up, nodded briefly as they went by and called Chap by name. "Make your orders quick today, will you, Chap? My one waitress is very busy."

"Sure thing, Mr. Coggins," Chap called.

They crowded in, pushing and shoving one another, and gave the waitress their orders—soft drinks, hamburgers, hot dogs, milk shakes, ham sandwiches—all the while carrying on a rapid-fire teasing and kidding that bewildered Katherine but didn't seem to bother the waitress one bit. When it was her turn to order, Katherine said, "Soup, please. And a green salad."

Chap looked at her. "Soup?"

"Why not?" she asked.

"Soup is what you eat when the family has left-overs and doesn't know what else to do with them."

Flip took up the game. "Soup is what you have when you're sick."

Red joined in. "Soup is dishwater with vegetables in it."

The waitress sighed wearily. "What you going to have, Miss?"

"Soup," said Katherine firmly.

"You see?" Troy laughed and looked fondly at Katherine as if she were some odd but cute thing. "The girl has a mind of her own and if she wants soup she'll have soup."

Binky bounced on the cushions of the booth. "What else

do you eat, Katherine? Snails—like they do in France? Tea and crumpets like in England? Frogs' legs?"

Katherine nodded. "Frogs' legs are delicious. My father likes them very much. I tried cooking them once but they weren't very good; I was much better at raviolis and lasagna and things like that." Then she added, "I ate little bits of octopus once, in a sort of rice and saffron dish they make around the Mediterranean. Paella, it's called."

She couldn't imagine what she had said that was so funny, yet they all laughed. Candy was gasping 'Octopus!' and laughing at the same time.

Then someone spoke, over her head. It was Jet, who had come up quietly and waited until he could be heard. "The question is not what she eats but what's her name. She can't go on being called Katherine. We'll have to think of something else for her."

A momentary panic seized Katherine. Why should they change her name, her clothes—tell her what to eat and what not to eat . . .

It was too late. No one listened to her feeble protest. "No, why should you? I don't want a different name!" Jet slid into the booth beside her and said, "How about Kay?" Flip shook her head. "Kit?" suggested Troy. "Kat?" was Pedro's suggestion. "Why not Puss—for octopus?" said Binky. They tossed the ideas around for a few minutes and then all decided on Kit. It was done! No matter what she thought of the idea, Katherine Norman was now Kit to the whole Crowd and there was nothing she could do about it.

Then Jet was talking to her, lowering his voice so that she had to bend to listen to him, making their conversation a little private. "What are you doing Saturday night?" he asked. "As a matter of fact, what are you doing tonight? We're all going over to Flip's and watch TV for a while and just horse around. How about it?"

"I can't," she told him. "I have a five-hundred-word paper to do for Miss Sunderman."

He started to argue with her, then shrugged his shoulders. "Okay. But how about Saturday night? We'll probably all go to a movie; we usually do. You're my date, you understand." He didn't smile. He was not being arrogant, overbold as he had been yesterday; only very serious and insistent. In that mood his personality was as attractive as his good looks, especially since she knew that what he was saying was *You belong with us, but with me particularly.* "Come on, Kit. Saturday night—seven-thirty?"

"Thank you, Jet. I'd like to. Very much," she answered.

He smiled then, took a bite out of his hamburger, stretched his long legs out under the table and leaned back against the booth. "Pedro," he called, "deal's on for Saturday night. Can you get your car? Will your folks let you have it?"

"I think so. You're a lucky man, Jet, to have your own."

"Lucky! I worked for two summers to get it. My Dad kept after me to put the money in the bank, save it for college, save it for my future. I told him I'd think about that when it came; what I needed was a car, right now."

"How will we work it for Saturday night?" Chap asked.

"Easy." It was obvious that if there was such a thing as a leader in this group it was Jet. He settled matters swiftly. "I'll pick up Kit and Troy; Chap, you be over at Troy's at seven-thirty. Pedro, you round up Binky, and Toby and Flip and Candy. Red lives only two blocks from the Alameda Theater and he can walk over and meet us there. Everybody got it? Good."

For some time Troy had been holding her sandwich in her hand, half-eaten, unaware of the rest of them, muttering to herself. They all seemed to look at her at the same moment. Chap nudged her. "What's with you? Have you gone into a trance?"

"'I cannot see what flowers are at my feet,'" she chanted.

" 'Nor what soft incense hangs upon the boughs.' I got it! I remembered." Then, looking at their puzzled faces, she laughed. "It's a stupid piece of poetry Kit and I have to memorize for today and I was saying it over to myself and I've got it down pat. Didn't I tell you what happened yesterday? Kit really put old Mailer in her place."

While she was telling the story, with slight exaggerations, Katherine had two thoughts: one, that it was nice of Troy to make her into a kind of heroine of the English Lit class; two, that Troy was a little ashamed of having been caught actually studying and that she was telling the story to divert attention away from herself.

Just then Flip happened to look up at the clock. "We're going to be late if we don't hurry."

As they all began piling out of the booth, Katherine saw something that stunned her. Underneath all the plates were heavy, red paper mats with FOOD SHOP and a fancy picture of a chef in a white cap printed on them. Jet slid one out from under Chap's plate and slipped it under his jacket. Not to be outdone, Chap grabbed a handful of paper napkins and stuffed them in his pocket. Flip, as they walked by the counter, took a quick look to be sure the waitress was not around and that the proprietor was busy taking money from Troy; then she lifted up the top of a straw container and pulled out six straws.

Outside on the sidewalk, a little away from the restaurant, they exhibited their treasures. "Four points for Flip!" . . . "Two for you, Chap; that's all. Napkins hardly count." It was Jet who was considered to have carried off the prize, because the mat had been difficult to conceal. "Ten points for a mat! I claim ten," he was determined, and Candy backed him up. "Jet should get ten. Pedro got six yesterday for that ash tray and that was easy to put into his pocket."

Troy saw the look on Katherine's face and laughed, taking her arm and pulling her away so that they were in the lead going back to school. "Don't give it a thought," she said. "It's only a game we started yesterday. Pedro put the ash tray back today. We're not really stealing anything. Jet will slip the mat back tomorrow. The napkins and straws are supposed to be free, anyway."

The cloud lifted and Katherine didn't give it another thought. It was just a game, as Troy said.

She saw Marguerite Kelley later that afternoon and began a hurried apology for not having lunch with her, but Marguerite cut her short. "Don't worry about it. Bob and I ate together. We looked all around for you; then we decided you'd gone to the Food Shop." Her voice was so cool that Katherine couldn't tell whether or not she was hurt.

Probably not. Probably both Bob and Marguerite were so busy and so wrapped up in their own affairs that it didn't really matter to either one of them if someone new, like herself, was with them. Bob had been kind to her, her first day in San Francisco. Marguerite had gone out of her way to be kind, her first day at school. However, it wasn't kindness that Katherine craved; it was to be wanted, to be accepted, to be a part of a group.

5

That day there were homework assignments from all of her classes and Miss Sunderman gave her another special paper to prepare, even though the first was not yet ready. A question in class revealed that Katherine had only the dimmest notion of the early religious struggles of the Puritans and that she had never heard of Cotton Mather or Roger Williams. "These juniors are far ahead of you," Miss Sunderman complained. "You'll just have to do a great deal more work to catch up."

It wasn't going to be as easy, in this American school, as Katherine had thought. The rest of the week was difficult, especially since Troy and Flip and Jet had a habit of telephoning her whenever they felt like it in the afternoons or evenings, demanding that she drop whatever she was doing and join them. She resisted as best she could, but one evening Troy and Binky and Flip descended on her. She had to study late that night to catch up and she was sleepy the next morning in class.

"Get this crazy room," Binky had marveled when she saw Katherine's bedroom. "I *like* it, but haven't you got a radio or a record player or anything?"

"It's absolutely elegant and it suits you, Kit," Flip enthused.

"There's a radio, a small one in the kitchen, that Aunt Debra said I could bring up here, but I haven't been able to decide whether I wanted it." She would have to, now. None of the Crowd seemed quite at ease unless music was blaring, as an accompaniment to their voices.

It was a wonderful thing that they liked her. She had come to realize that it was not easy to be accepted by this group; they were a tight circle and they kept to themselves. Why did they like her? she wondered. They seemed to think the things she said and did were "cute," but she was quickly learning that she mustn't be too different. Basically she must think and do as they did.

She must not say no every time they telephoned, nor did she want to; but to keep up with the Crowd and her studies was difficult. Grudgingly she found herself being grateful for the schedule on the closet door. Much as she hated it, it had a way of organizing her time. She couldn't daydream so long as it was there, poking and prodding and haunting her.

The one real cloud over her happiness was Bob Macdonald. He spoke to her at school; but he was always in a hurry, always rushing some place. He hadn't asked her for a date, as Jet had. Perhaps, in America, if you were friends with a sister, you could not be friends with her brother? Katherine puzzled over this. No, it was probably the school newspaper that took up all his time.

She thought it silly. This was only a school, so it could not be a real newspaper. It was all a pretense, this newspaper and the clubwork Marguerite Kelley took so seriously. Only the Crowd saw through the pretense and would have nothing to do with it.

Katherine had made up her mind about Aunt Debra too. I'll not think about her. I'll speak to her when I have to and forget her as much as possible. After all, that's the way she treats me. When Katherine spoke to her, sometimes, of something that deeply interested her, Debra Norman looked startled and disturbed. As if I were a fly that had accidentally gotten into her soup, Katherine thought.

No, Debra Norman set a pattern and Katherine followed it. A few remarks at breakfasttime: "Did you sleep well? Did you get your homework done last night?" and at dinnertime the same sort of thing: "How was school? Are you going to wash that blouse? Don't use up all the hot water tonight."

She doesn't really want to know anything about me, Katherine decided. Very well, I won't tell her anything.

Once in a while, though, Katherine caught a glimpse of an Aunt Debra who was a stranger. These were the rare times when the older woman spoke of her work. Then her long, rather horsy face became animated and alive and Katherine saw a quick picture of a busy office, a bustling, chic hotel world where her aunt obviously held a position of some importance. Just when she would come to something interesting, Aunt Debra would break off and say, "Oh, that wouldn't interest you. Why should I bother you with it?"

Katherine would have liked to hear more. The Marlborough's temperamental desk clerk had just insulted the new hotel guest and now she'd never know what happened after that. If her aunt didn't want to tell her, she certainly wasn't going to insist with questions.

Saturday morning was lovely. Katherine slept late. When she came downstairs the cleaning woman, Mrs. Nocke, was already there and giving the living room what she called a "good turning out."

"Hurry with your breakfast, Katherine," her aunt ordered. "Then collect your towels and sheets and any of your clothes that don't need to be washed by hand. We'll drive over and take the laundry to the Quick-Wash."

The Quick-Wash was a place of fascination for Katherine. "Why, I've never seen anything like this," she exclaimed as she and Miss Norman sorted the clothes, placing the sheets in one machine, the smaller white linen in another, the colored clothes in another. "You mean it all is done automatically? We just put in our quarters and go away and leave it?" She fastened the doors, with their glass fronts, and begged, "Please, let me pour the soap in. One-half cupful in each?"

"Katherine! These aren't playthings. They're very efficient machines. We'll go do the marketing now; come back in an hour and these will be ready for the dryers." Impatiently she pulled at Katherine's arm. "Are you going to stay here all day just looking at the clothes tumble around in soapy water?"

"I could. It's as much fun as watching television." She let herself be led away and, once she was in the supermarket, she forgot all about the Quick-Wash. She was completely dazzled. "I used to think it was exciting," she said as she pushed the wire cart up one aisle and down the next, "to visit the outdoor markets and stalls in Italy. Once Daddy even took me into the bazaars in Tangier. But this! Everything in the world is here—Oh, I could cook such wonderful things if you'd let me. Look, there's brown rice and soy sauce and all those wonderful spices. Aunt Debra, do you know you don't even have oregano or rosemary or garlic in your house? You *need* them."

Her aunt scarcely heard her. She was frowning over the list in her hand, checking off items. "What? Oh, nonsense. Salt and pepper and a bay leaf is all we need for a good stew." She happened to look up then and saw Katherine's face. "You look as if you'd been invited to a party and didn't have a present. Buy your precious oregano and those other things if you want them so much."

They were so late over the shopping—"dawdling," her aunt called it—that by the time they reached home Katherine had just time enough to wash her face, brush her hair and put on a little lipstick before Troy and Flip and Candy arrived.

Now there was more shopping, this time in downtown San Francisco at the Collegiate Shop. "We'll go to the big department stores later," Troy told her. They crowded into the small shop where the owner, a young and clever woman, took one look at Katherine and said, "Red hair. Blue eyes. Hmmm—why no freckles? And you have dark eyebrows, not the usual light ones that redheads have. Let's see—you can wear greens and blues and some browns. Black. Yes, black. No pinks or anything with a purple tone."

Troy held up a cinnamon-colored sweater. "This has a little

66

pink cast to it but I have a hunch it would be sensational on Kit. Try it on, please."

The shopowner looked doubtful, but when Katherine came out of the cubicle wearing the sweater she agreed it was sensational. "Any time you want a job working for me, Troy Macdonald," she said, "you can have it, with your eye for color combinations. You're an artist."

With the cinnamon sweater went a matching skirt; for the skirt, also, there was a white blouse and a tailored green one with a high, flaring collar. Katherine couldn't resist any of them although the prices made her feel weak at the knees. Without the twenty dollars her aunt had insisted on giving her before she left the house, she couldn't possibly have managed. For the first time since she had come to San Francisco her feeling for Debra Norman was something a good deal more than just dutiful.

She did say no to another skirt. "I have a green suit, a tweed one, and I can wear that skirt to school some of the time."

"You will have to have a dress for parties and dances and things like that," said Binky.

They looked over all the party dresses, with their wide, swirling skirts, and then Katherine shook her head. "I brought with me yards and yards of Italian silk and if I have a pattern I can make one just like these. It's a blue and black plaid, with a cream stripe in it and it's beautiful. So all I need to buy is the black patent-leather belt to go with it and a crinoline petticoat."

Purchases in hand, they went to the department stores—not so much to buy as to look; to ride the escalators and sniff longingly at the perfume counters and try on the bracelets and earrings at the jewelry counters, where Flip did buy one more charm for her bracelet. Next they spent an hour in the department where records were sold and they all crowded into one booth to listen; then out to another department store where the main attraction was the soda-fountain–restaurant that sold special ice creams.

They went back to Troy's house afterward, a little tired, ready to sprawl out in the living room and just talk.

"What movie are we seeing tonight?" asked Troy.

"I don't know." Binky was sitting on the floor with her shoes off, wiggling her tired toes. "I wish sometimes *we* could pick one out. It's always Jet who says we'll go to the Alameda tonight, or the Monterey or wherever he decides."

"The Alameda is closest and it's easier because Candy and Red can walk there and we don't have to spend so much time running around in the cars, picking each other up," Troy explained.

"Well, Red is not going to pick me up tonight, I can tell you that." Candy's outburst matched the sulky expression on her face. "Red and I are through. We don't even *like* each other very much, yet we've had to go steady just because the rest of you paired us off. George Yale has asked me for a date for tonight and I'm going with him and if you want to include him in, okay. If not, I'll go out with him alone."

Flip and Troy and Binky stared at her, shocked. Flip said, "Oh, Candy. George Yale is a drip. I know he's crazy about you and he's been trying to horn in on our Crowd for a long time, but we don't like him. And what about Red?"

"If Jet could lone-wolf it in the Crowd, why can't Red?" Candy asked. "As for George, if you want me you'll have to take him, that's all."

Troy got up from her chair and sat on the arm of the sofa, next to Candy. She slid her hand in a quick, downward motion past Candy's face. "Wipe off the frown. Of course we'll take him if you want him. We may even like him; there are probably unexplored depths in George Yale we don't know anything about."

This made Binky giggle. The tense moment had passed.

At home Katherine found the house sparklingly clean. Aunt Debra, in a tailored woolen housecoat, just up from a nap, looked more relaxed, more pleasant, than she had all week.

She greeted Katherine with something that was almost a smile. "Your date has been calling all afternoon. He finally left a message about three o'clock and said he would be busy until six but would call you then, and could you be ready by eight o'clock tonight."

"Jet?"

"Jet? Who is that? Is that a name? No, I mean Bob Macdonald."

Katherine felt a strange tremor run all along her nerves, a burst of wonderful excitement—and a sinking of dismay. Bob had called—not just once, but over and over. It must mean that he wanted to see her, but she had a date which couldn't be broken.

"He's not my date. Jet is—his real name is John Smith but his nickname is Jet," she explained to her aunt. When she saw the alarmed look on Debra Norman's face, she quickly added, "He's a friend of Troy's. It's quite all right, really."

"I suppose so," dubiously. "This problem of young men coming to see you and taking you out—I might as well tell you that's been bothering me ever since I knew you were coming here. I'll trust your judgment as much as I can, but I do wish it were Bob. I know him."

At six o'clock sharp the telephone rang. It was Bob. "I'm sorry, Katherine, that I couldn't reach you earlier. I should have called you last night. How does this sound? We'll grab a cable car up to nearly the top of Powell, walk down to Grant and I'll show you Chinatown at night. Then we can decide from there what we want to do—go to a movie or just drift around. I can introduce you to some wonderful characters I know here."

"I can't, Bob. I'm going out with the Crowd."

There was silence for a few seconds. Then he said, slowly, "You mean you're going out with Jet, don't you? What do you want to go out with him for? He's not your type."

Her temper flared. "He asked me days ago. He didn't wait until today, that's why."

"Okay, I'm sorry. I just got so busy, so wound up with all this work trying to get the first issue of the *Bridge* sewed up that I didn't have a moment. Honestly. I thought we'd celebrate. I was picked as editor yesterday." Bob's voice had gone flat with disappointment. "I guess there's nothing more to be said, is there? If you want that Crowd, that lets me out." He hung up.

I guess that lets me out, too, she thought. She hung onto her temper, repeating to herself, Why didn't he call earlier? Is his stupid old newspaper so important he couldn't have thought about me before? However, not even temper could blur the disappointment she was feeling. A cable-car ride and a walk to Chinatown might not be the most glamorous of evenings, but with Bob it would be. He made it sound magical and marvelous; whether that was part of his nature or the magic was just for her, she didn't know. She only knew she was torn between two strong emotions: wanting to be alone with Bob and wanting not to be alone but with the Crowd.

At seven-thirty Jet was on the Norman porch, ringing the doorbell. The hallway was dimly lit when she introduced him to Aunt Debra and the older woman peered at him, under and over her glasses, until Katherine was embarrassed and Jet jammed his hands in his pockets with a truculent air. All Aunt Debra said, however, was "It's nice meeting you, Mr. Smith. Be sure that Katherine is back before twelve o'clock."

Outside the door he let out his breath. "What an old battle-ax! She was really giving me the third degree, looking me over, wasn't she? How do you stand living with a woman like that?"

"If you are going to be rude about her, then I'll stay home." It was one thing for her to criticize Debra Norman. No outsider could.

He laughed and hustled her to the car, where Chap and Troy were already sitting in the back seat. "I should have known that red hair had a temper with it. So all right, she's beautiful. Who cares?"

The double bill at the theater had a war picture and a tender love story. During the first one, Jet whispered a lot to Pedro, who was sitting on the other side of him; but during the love story he moved so that his arm touched Katherine's, and then he tried to hold her hand.

"Don't," she said.

"Why not?" He moved slightly away but soon he had captured her hand again, holding it so tight she would have had to struggle and pull and tug to stop him. So she let it be.

When it was over they piled, all of them, into the two cars and went to a drive-in for sandwiches. It was Katherine's first experience at this kind of open-air restaurant where food was brought to the cars, and she was fascinated—so much so that she forgot she was provoked at Jet for holding her hand.

"You mean you've never done this before?" he asked.

"Never. There are lots of cafés in Europe where you sit at little tables on the sidewalk and watch people going by, but who ever thought of having your sandwich brought to your car?" She thought it was marvelous, watching the car on the other side of them; the way the waitress fitted the trays over the doors and over the steering wheel.

There were so many of them that George Yale and Candy had had to split up. George was in front with Katherine and Jet, and now he was saying, "Oh, that's crazy. What are you getting so excited about? It's only a drive-in."

Jet turned and looked beyond Katherine at George. It was a long, hard stare. "That's one of the reasons I like her. Everybody's bored but Kit. This girl's been all over the world, to places you never heard of, but she can still get excited because she sees a waitress fix a tray to a car door."

"Sure. Sure, Jet," George mumbled.

Katherine understood, then, why the Crowd had so little use for George Yale. He was too anxious to agree with Jet; too eager to please Jet; too eager to belong. While Jet reached out and turned on the car radio, one part of her mind listened to the music but the other part was listening to George as he leaned back to talk to Candy and Troy and Chap in the back seat. It was the same thing: whatever they said he agreed with; if he made a statement which they didn't like, he hastily contradicted himself.

The whole Crowd, she thought, is apt to have pretty much the same ideas, but this George Yale doesn't have *any* mind of his own.

The music was good and Jet turned the dial up louder and louder. In the car on their left was an elderly couple; they both craned their necks and glared at Jet. The waitress came over.

"I'm sorry," she said, "but you'll have to turn that down a little. It's blaring all over the place and people are complaining that they can't talk or think or eat in comfort."

Jet looked at her, grinned and pantomimed, holding his hand behind his ear. "What?" he shouted. "I can't hear you." He made no move toward the radio. The waitress left.

"Turn it down, please," Katherine asked.

"Oh, no. We have just as much right to play it as the rest have *not* to play theirs. It's a free country."

The waitress had gone over to speak to a tall, burly, broad-shouldered man and now he walked to the car and stood at the window, looking at Jet. "The girl asked you to turn down your radio," he said in a calm voice. "I'm the manager here. I run a quiet, nice, respectable place. You are disturbing other people. Either do as we ask, or leave." Seeing that Jet made no move, the manager suddenly reached in and turned the dial off. In the abrupt silence Katherine could hear Jet breathing fast. He and the manager had locked glances and both were absolutely still.

With a quick, abrupt motion Jet's hands went to the handle of the door; the manager was even quicker—and stronger. Like lightning, he had both of Jet's hands pinned down, hard, with his two larger ones.

"That will be enough of that," he said, still quiet and calm. "You'd like to get out and take a swing at me but you aren't going to. You're going to turn that ignition key on, back out slowly and go some place else. I don't want you here."

"I'm sitting down and you're standing up," Jet flung the angry words at him. "You've got me at a disadvantage. There's an empty lot in back of this drive-in where no one can see us. I'll take you on there in a fair fight."

The manager shook his head. "Wish I could oblige you, friend, but I can't. I'm an ex-prize fighter and I still box once in a while professionally. The law puts boxers in a special category. Under the law my fist is classed as a weapon, just like a gun or a club. If I hit you and hurt you, I'd go to prison for assault with a deadly weapon. Now just behave and get out." So sure was he of his own strength and authority that he released Jet's wrists and walked away, turning his back to them unconcernedly.

Katherine, who had been sitting panic-stricken during this exchange, felt the tension in Jet's body and the slight move he made toward the door and the handle. She couldn't say anything but she was praying: *Don't! Don't get out and make trouble.*

Then George Yale spoke up. "Go on, Jet! Force him to meet you in the lot in back. Chap and I'll circle around the other side and then all three of us can jump him."

"That's crazy," came from Chap in the back seat. The car was a two-door sedan and, during the altercation with the manager, Chap could not get out. He had moved, once, to help Jet and had been squelched by the solid bulk of the older man and by a swift warning glance from his eyes. "That's real crazy," he repeated.

"Yeah." Tension flowed out of Jet and he relaxed back against the seat. He even grinned. "I'll fight my own battles, George, thank you. And I'm not dope enough to tangle with a prize fighter. Come on. Yell out to Pedro." Pedro and Flip and those in the other car were some distance away; they had been watching the disturbance with bewilderment and making signs to ask what was going on. "Give him the word and then let's roll. We'll go to the Frenchman's."

Katherine could feel the relief, the release of pent-up breathing, from the back seat. "Good boy, Jet. That's using your head; you're playing it smart," said Chap admiringly.

"And you challenged him." There was almost hero worship in Candy's voice. "Big as he was, you offered to fight him."

Was Jet a hero? To the Crowd he obviously was. Brave and smart. Katherine was weak and trembling, now that it was all over, and her mind was as shaken as her nerves. Was Jet a hero? she wondered. Were these the right standards and values in America? She didn't know. It just seemed to her that there was a flaw in this somewhere.

"Scared?" He looked at her as they drove away. "You don't ever need to be scared when you're with me, Kit. I don't often get into fights and I'm not so dumb I'd get into one where I didn't have a chance. Don't let it spoil your evening."

She said soberly, "I was more than just scared. I was very frightened."

He pulled her over toward him, slightly. He said in a low voice that held laughter in it, "You know something? So was I. But don't tell anyone."

Then she liked him again. In the back seat Troy began to sing and Candy joined in. To them this had just been an incident and now it was over. Katherine's own spirits lightened and brightened. The evening had been threatened, but now it was all right and no harm had been done and she could relax and enjoy herself. At the Frenchman's, another drive-in, they found only three other cars besides their two; all were filled with young people and no one objected to the music—though Katherine noticed that Jet was playing it much more softly.

74

When he drove her home, after Chap and Troy left to cross the street, he asked her, "Have a good time?"

"I had a lovely time. You know, now that—that trouble is all over it just seems rather exciting and not frightening." She leaned forward to look at all the chrome and fixtures on the dashboard. "This is a nice car you have, Jet."

"It should be. I saved every penny and worked summers at the Marlborough to get it."

"At the Marlborough?" She stared at him. "Why, that's where my Aunt Debra works. You do mean the hotel, don't you?"

He whistled. "That's where I've seen her before. I thought there was something familiar about her but it was too dark in your hallway to see her clearly. Sure she works there; she's the secretary to the manager. In fact, she carries as much weight around there as the big boss, himself." He got out and came around to open the door for her. They walked slowly up to the porch saying nothing. He was thoughtful, considering something before he spoke.

Finally, at the steps, he said, "Look, Kit—you'll probably hear some gossip about me from your aunt, if she happens to remember who I am. She may not; there are a lot of employees and she may not remember that I was a bellhop there last summer. If she does, don't you believe the story. It's not true. I got fired from the Marlborough because the head bellhop had it in for me and he claimed I stole a woman's purse." The outrage in Jet's voice was sincere. "I never saw that purse—and a month later, after I was fired, they had a letter from the woman apologizing because she hadn't lost it at all. It was her change purse and she found it in another bag, at home. You have to believe me."

"Of course I believe you. Why shouldn't I? I couldn't imagine you stealing anyone's purse." When he tried to kiss her she pulled away and ran past him to the door. "See you Monday," she called softly.

Once again, the next morning, she was allowed to sleep late and breakfast was on the table when she came down. "It's a beautiful day," her aunt said. "No fog. You haven't seen our famous foggy days, when they come one after another and you can hardly see across the street. We'll take advantage of the sunshine today and do a little sight-seeing. First, though, I must stop in at the hotel. Mr. Dale called. He can't find a paper which I know I handed to him on Friday night."

So first they drove to Nob Hill. Katherine's eyes widened at the sight of the entrance to the hotel, with its semi-circle driveway and the lordly doorman in the green coat and gold braid, the immense lobby and its marble pillars and thick green rugs and wine-colored sofas and deep chairs. Aunt Debra wasn't impressed; she was right at home. She made her way briskly to the elevator, past the reception desk. The reception clerk bowed to her. "Good morning, Miss Norman." The elevator man took her to the mezzanine without asking. He, too, was polite and deferential. "Nice day, isn't it, Miss Norman? It's too bad you have to come in on a Sunday."

Sunday or not, there were people working in the mezzanine offices. A hotel must operate seven days and nights a week. A very young stenographer raised startled, scared eyes when Miss Norman appeared, and hastily put away a magazine and rattled a sheet of paper into her typewriter. "Hello, Miss Norman," she said. "Mr. Dale isn't here just now. But the housekeeper is in an awful state; she says there are four sheets missing from her supply-room inventory."

"Thank you, Dora," Debra Norman's voice was crisp. "Phone her and tell her to come up immediately and see me. I'll be in Mr. Dale's office. Have you finished yesterday's report? Good. I need it. And ask Mr. Rogers, from Maintenance, to call me if he's in the basement. One of the guests, in Room 645, complained yesterday that the hot water is not running properly; it just trickles out. That's the third complaint from that floor this month. Mr. Rogers will have to do something more than just tinker with it." She glanced at the report the stenographer had handed her. "Oh, good girl. You've done it just right."

Then her aunt turned to Katherine. "If you'd like to sit here and wait I'll get a magazine for you. Or would you rather wander about in the lobby? I can have you paged from there."

More amazing than the beauty and splendor of the hotel, Katherine thought as she roamed about, was the change in her aunt's behavior . . . the difference between Debra Norman here in the hotel and Debra Norman at home. No, that was wrong. Her behavior and manner *weren't* different. It was just that it was the proper kind of manner for a working situation, for an office, for an executive secretary, and the same manner didn't belong in a home. Her briskness and authority were something to be admired here, while at home they set Katherine's teeth on edge.

While she walked along a charming gallery lined with shops displaying expensive merchandise of cashmere sweaters and brocaded evening dresses, expensive bric-a-brac, a flower shop . . . Katherine was really puzzling over this personality of her aunt's. It's because, she suddenly realized, Aunt Debra's real life is spent here at the hotel. Her house has become just a place to eat and sleep in. All of her interests are centered here; it must have been more of a wrench than Daddy and I knew for her to take me in and try to change the pattern of her life by adjusting to me.

With this new knowledge Katherine made a firm resolve to try to understand her Aunt Debra better and to be more sympathetic to her. Actually she was feeling proud of her aunt. Everyone in the hotel seemed to admire "Miss Norman" and to look up to her and defer to her and bring all their problems to her. She must be really very capable and more of an assistant to the manager than a secretary.

Three-quarters of an hour later her aunt found her. Her car

77

was brought to the door and soon they were winding their way eastward through the city, making so many left and right turns that Katherine became completely lost. Then they were climbing, circling and winding up a hill until they reached the park of Buena Vista. They stopped the car on the crest and got out to look at the city, the ocean and the bay.

6

Katherine caught her breath. Not in all the world had she seen anything lovelier than this. "Not on the Riviera, nor any place else," she said, dazed.

"It is beautiful, isn't it?" her aunt said, almost surprised. "It's been years and years since I've been up here. I almost forgot what a sight it is. I get into such a rut, running back and forth between office and home, I just don't do the things I really want to."

Below them the hills of San Francisco rose, sloped down, rose again, and all the hills were covered with houses or tall buildings so that red roofs, gray roofs, toy white buildings and majestic towers of buildings were a riot of pattern and color. Here and there the dark green of gardens and parks and trees wove a darker stitching into the tapestry. It was the bay, so very blue, that was the greatest wonder of all. Great white or gray ships slid into the bay; tiny sailboats were flicks of movement and color on its surface; far across it were islands; to the right was the solid, low-set curve of the Bay Bridge and to the left the dazzling wonder of the Golden Gate Bridge, so slim, so delicate, so strong in its arch below and its tall spires above.

The wind was blowing into their faces. It disturbed the set severity of the hair on Debra Norman's forehead and softened the boniness of her features. Even her voice was gentler as she pointed out places of interest to her niece. "That's Mare Island. And that's the Presidio, where the army post has been located since your great-grandfather's day. Across the bay, to your right, is the city of Berkeley, where the University of California is located."

As they were climbing back into the car, Aunt Debra commented on Katherine's cinnamon-colored sweater. "Is that one of your new purchases? It's very nice."

Conscience-stricken, Katherine stared at the older woman. "I never showed them to you, did I? After you were so nice and gave me money to help buy them. Oh, please forgive me. It was thoughtless and wrong of me."

"I did wonder a little, yesterday. But if you have the grace to apologize, Katherine, it's almost as good as if you had remembered in the first place. To admit you are wrong about something is just as difficult at your age as it is at mine."

From the park they drove down through the city's business section and on to where Aunt Debra indicated another hill. "That's Telegraph," she said. "Many artists and writers live there. Also there are fine restaurants in this section."

Fisherman's Wharf, when they reached it and parked, was pure delight. Noisy, smelling of fish; raucous with men in white aprons shouting at them to come and buy their marvelous lobsters, their excellent crabs, their perfect shrimps—"Look, Lady! Come and buy—nice abalone shells for souvenirs! Use them for ash trays. Picture postcards of the cable cars and the wharf!" It was gay and colorful, crowded and friendly.

Restaurants were a solid line, fronting on the sidewalk, but Aunt Debra said it was early and she took her niece through a narrow alleyway back of the restaurants to where the fishing boats were tied up, one next to the other, in a square-shaped lagoon of water. As they watched them bobbing up and down to the gentle swell, they chose favorites. "I like the blue and white *Maria*. It's so clean and so pretty," Katherine said.

Debra Norman preferred the larger *Napoli II*, where a fisherman was mending a huge net and a young man was helping him, both seated on a wooden box. "I like that one. If this is the second *Napoli*, it shows tradition. The father was probably a fisherman; perhaps even the grandfather, and the business and the knowledge and love of the seat were handed down from generation to generation. That's a good way of life— Why, that young man sitting there—he's no fisherman. That's Bob Macdonald, as sure as I'm standing here. What do you suppose he's doing?"

"Bob!" Katherine called.

The young man who had been mending the net half rose from the wooden box. He shaded his eyes to see who was calling. Then he came quickly, climbing up to the pier beside them. "Hello, Aunt Debra. Hi, Katherine. I've been visiting with a friend of mine, Mr. Antonelli."

"I never saw such a boy, with friends all over the city." Miss Norman shook her head. "Is there any hole or corner of San Francisco you haven't wandered into and found friends, Bob? I remember when you were little your mother used to say you knew every storekeeper by name, the policemen in the neighborhood, the firemen in the firehouse—"

He colored a little. "I get a kick out of it. That's why I want to be a newspaperman someday. I like to wander around and get people's stories and find out what they do and what they think."

Miss Norman rubbed her nose. "It's lunch time and I'm sure Katherine is hungry. I know I am. Come and have some sea food with us, Bob. I haven't seen much of you these late years, but you used to have an enormous appetite—we could never fill you up."

He hesitated, looking at Katherine.

Her heart was pounding and it was with an unsteady voice that she said, "Please do. It would be nice, having you."

Not only was it exciting to be with Bob but he was a great help in another way, too. He smoothed out some of the stiffness between her and Aunt Debra and—perhaps because she had such affectionate memories of him and Troy as children—he was able to make her talk more easily. Under his teasing she even laughed once or twice, that quick, abrupt, snorting laugh of hers.

"Sea food for brains, indeed!" she scoffed. "Who ever told you such a silly thing about sea food being brain food? If that were true, then San Franciscans should be among the smartest people in the world; we certainly eat enough of it."

"We are the smartest, you know that." He pretended to be serious. "Aren't we the smartest people in the whole world, Katherine?"

"Oh, I've met a few others," Katherine retorted.

"Listen to who's bragging," said her aunt.

They had both spoken at the same time and now they exchanged an amused glance, saying to each other that you couldn't take Bob Macdonald seriously when he was in this mood.

"Traitors," he judged them both. He was eating Crab Louie and now he speared a big chunk of crabmeat on his fork and slid it onto Katherine's plate. "Eat that and tell me if you ever tasted anything better. Maybe we aren't so smart here but we know good food."

"Mmmm. Wonderful." Katherine tasted and agreed. "I'd love to get the recipe for that and make some."

"You can cook, *too?*"

Debra Norman and her niece looked down at their plates and avoided each other's eyes. This was a sensitive subject. They were both remembering the burned waffles.

Bob was intent for a while on his lunch, then he changed the subject. "How do you like Golden Gate High School by now, Katherine? How do you like an American school?"

"It sounded too easy at first but I'm finding I have to work very hard, especially on this American history. The first report I handed in to Miss Sunderman wasn't very good because, she said, I hadn't done enough background reading and didn't really understand what I was saying. She scared me a little; she's so snappish and she says just what she thinks. But the second one she liked a lot. She said it was extremely well written and original."

"How do you mean—original?" her aunt asked.

Katherine stammered a little. Her aunt had never shown any such interest before. "I—I was tired of just saying that Cotton Mather believed so and so and did so and so and that Roger Williams was chased out of one colony into another for his religious beliefs. So I thought I'd try something new. I made it a debate, an imaginary debate, between the two men and they argued out what each one believed."

"That was a swell idea," Bob approved.

"That's just the sort of thing your father would have done," Aunt Debra added. "Even as a boy in school, his compositions had a certain flair and sparkle to them."

"It must be tough on you," Bob said, "coming into a strange school and trying to catch up. If I hadn't been so busy maybe I could have helped you, but the first week is always a bad one when you're trying to get a newspaper started. I'd finish my homework every night and then rough out a story idea or an editorial, and I'd plan to call you to see how you were getting along; but by the time I finished I was so bushed I couldn't think of anything but getting some sleep. Do you remember, Aunt Debra, how you used to paddle us on our birthdays— one for each year and one to grow on? You should have hit me harder instead of tapping me so gently; then maybe I'd be over six feet tall and big as a football player and have more energy."

"You're tall enough, for heaven's sake," she answered. "Why don't you get some fat on you? I remember those birthday parties. Your mother used to get me to come over and manage you kids while you played games, like pinning the tail on the donkey—"

"Do you remember when I got turned around and jabbed the pin into that blonde kid—what was her name?—with all that long hair?" Bob asked, laughing.

"I certainly do. She yelled and screamed and told her mother that you had tried to kill her." Debra Norman was smiling now. "What a time I had that day, with that child screaming and you scowling at her and Theresa crying that her party was being ruined. I remember I gave the child a prize in the next game and then she calmed down, until her mother came for her and she started screaming all over again."

Katherine just listened, wondering. It was almost impossible to think of her aunt at a children's party.

Before Bob left to go back and join his fisherman friend, he asked Katherine, "How would you like to come up to the fourth floor tomorrow after school and see the offices of the *Bridge?*"

"I'd like to," she said promptly. "Thanks a lot."

Going home, Aunt Debra still pursued the thought which Bob's mention of birthday parties had brought up. "I just hadn't realized until now," she said, "how many friends I've lost track of and how many things I used to do that I don't do any more. It's true that my work is exhausting but, still, I have gotten into a rut. I should make an effort to change." She glanced sideways at Katherine, beside her in the car. "Perhaps your coming to live with me—oh, that idiot!" She wrenched the wheel of the car and turned it sharply to the right. "Did you see that? He cut right in front of me."

Katherine peered out of the windshield. She wished Aunt Debra had finished what she was about to say; it had sounded hopeful. She looked again and recognized the car, now directly in front of them.

"Why, that's Jet's car!" she exclaimed. "That was Jet—the friend you met the other night."

"Friend, huh. He's an unmannerly fool and shouldn't be allowed to drive a car. I wouldn't want to think you were riding with him if he did something like that again. What did you say his name was? It sounds very peculiar."

They had come to the house and Aunt Debra braked and stopped.

"Jet Smith. His real name is John Smith." Katherine climbed out and followed her aunt into the house. "I introduced you to him. He said he used to work at the Marlborough in the summers, as a bellboy."

They were in the hallway now and Debra Norman turned abruptly to face her niece. "You mean *that* John Smith? I most certainly do remember now. It wasn't very light in the hallway last night but there *was* something vaguely familiar about him. There should be," she said grimly, "he caused us enough trouble. Katherine, I don't want you seeing that boy or going out with him again."

"What?" Katherine was jolted out of her absorption in unbuttoning her jacket. "Why shouldn't I see him? He told me about his being fired, but he also said the charge against him was false."

"So it was," Miss Norman admitted. The lines around her mouth had tightened and she looked sternly at her niece. "That's not the point. If it had been any other employee of the hotel, we would not have fired him without a great deal of investigation. The trouble with boys like that John Smith is they do small, petty things that ruin your confidence in them so that when some big thing happens you're ready to believe the worst. He was smart-alecky, impudent to the other employees and the guests; he thought he was too good to work hard or work well. The worst of it was that he had boasted about taking little things—such as hotel stationery. The stationery is free to the guests but the employees know that it costs the hotel money and we aren't supposed to use it. So when the purse was stolen we jumped to the conclusion he had done it."

"You admit you were wrong!" Katherine's voice was rising in indignation. "You admit he was falsely accused. Yet now you say I can't see him, just as if he really were the thief."

"Don't raise your voice to me." Debra Norman's foot began to tap the floor in agitation. She took off her coat and hung it up. Her back was rigid and stiff. "I don't like that tone of voice from a young girl. It isn't respectful. At my age it's just too much responsibility to have to worry over you going out with the wrong kind of boy. He's no proper person for you to associate with; he's undisciplined. I don't say he is a bad one. I do say he is a troublemaker. I forbid you to see him."

"My father never forbade me to do anything. We always talked things out until we agreed." Anger was a throbbing vein in Katherine's forehead. She was shaking all over. "I'm not ten years old. Why do you treat me as if I were?"

"Because you are acting like it. Go to your room, please, until you are over this tantrum."

Katherine turned her back and started up the stairs.

Her aunt had the Norman temper, too, and now it flared. "And don't be always telling me what your father would do. I know Cyrus Norman as well as you do; he's my brother as well as your father." She stood with her hands on her hips. "I thought this afternoon I was going to be glad you came. You were a very nice girl. But if I have to put up with this kind of adolescent nonsense, and you past the age for that— Katherine! Do you hear me?"

But the girl had run up the stairs and banged her bedroom door shut, cutting off the sound of Aunt Debra's voice.

Hateful. That's what she was. Just hateful! A tyrant. Katherine kicked the bedpost. She flung herself flat on the bed and pounded the pillow. Troy had been right when she said adults in authority demanded that you act like a grownup one minute, and the next treated you like a child.

I am acting like a child, she thought, but I can't help it. Her fury cooled, even though the anger remained. It had been completely unfair of her aunt to condemn Jet, when she knew he had not been guilty of what the Marlborough had accused him of—stealing. Her aunt had no right to pass judgment on him and forbid her to see him.

The very fact that he was forbidden made him seem more glamorous in Katherine's eyes and, without actually coming to a decision, she knew she was not going to obey Aunt Debra.

So her aunt had thought this afternoon that she was going

to be glad Katherine had come, because Katherine had seemed like a nice girl! I thought I was going to be glad, too. I thought she was beginning to act human and kind and that she had a sense of humor. But it was just because it was a holiday, as if she had put on a Sunday dress; underneath, she is still the same old Aunt Debra.

It bothered her that Bob Macdonald liked her aunt. Why should he? She tried to imagine her aunt at a children's birthday party, playing games and laughing, ladling out ice cream into the children's bowls. . . . Katherine gave it up, shaking her head. It was impossible to imagine.

After she had calmed down, she managed to study a little. Her aunt passed her door and called in, "I'm going to bed early and read. Your dinner is down on the table. Don't sulk; you must eat. I hope by tomorrow you can apologize."

Behind the closed door Katherine didn't even answer. She made another Italian gesture and if Miss Mailer had seen that one she would have known it was rude.

The next day, after her last class, Katherine walked up to the fourth floor and visited the editorial offices of the *Bridge*. In one corner of the room, as she hesitated in the doorway, she saw a girl clattering away at a typewriter; at another desk a boy with a shock of untidy curly hair was scribbling away, stopping every now and then to bite the end of his pencil or run his hands through his hair, making it more untidy than ever. Bob was seated behind the biggest desk and in front of it a very fat boy was showing him some cartoon sketches for approval.

The fat boy was disgusted. He couldn't say ten words without being interrupted by the other two reporters.

"Bob," the girl called out, "this story on the Drama Club . . . do you want me to run down and get a personal quote from the president of the club?"

"You do that, Audrey." This was a different Bob from the relaxed and carefree young man on the wharf yesterday; here was a dynamo of action. "You do that. Ask the president and *pin him down*—for the name of the play they're going to do and who is going to have the principal lead. Don't let him stall you." He turned back to the artist. "Now about this one cartoon—"

"Bob"—the other reporter had by now made a real rat's nest out of his hair—"someone's handed in the names of the football team and I know most of them aren't spelled right. Shall I go hunt up the coach or the players or—"

"Don't waste the time." Bob managed to do three things at once: wave to Katherine to come on in, shake his head no over the sketch he was holding, and answer the reporter's question. "Don't go chasing around when last year's yearbook's right over there. All you have to do is look up the names; they were either on the team last year or in the second string. I think there's only one new one, a transfer from Los Angeles and you can get his name from Mr. Johns."

"Are you or aren't you going to pick out one of these cartoons?" the fat boy protested.

"Simmer down. Sure I am. Be with you in a minute, Katherine. Now—this one of the football coach is the best, I think. Leave it here and I'll think up a caption for it. What about next week? Can't you give me something really funny? Something like that one you did last year, about the cafeteria? Remember? You had animals' faces on all the kids and we called it 'The Zoo at Feeding Time.'"

"Okay, Bob. I'll think of something." The fat boy went away.

The girl called Audrey had gone and the blond boy was over by the bookshelf, muttering to himself as he copied down names from the yearbook. For a little while the office was quiet. Bob came from behind his desk, put Katherine's books down on a table and guided her around. "These are all the stacked copies of last year's *Bridge*," he explained, showing her a neat pile. "These cartoons on the walls are some of the best ones from past years. They give us something to shoot for. On this table we collect the newspapers from other high schools, so we can steal ideas from them. Sometimes they steal from us, too. The *Bridge* has three reporters. When they actually finish their copy, it goes into this basket. In that other basket go suggestions, ideas, notes from me to them and from them to me. That's our working basket," referring to the shallow wire basket on his desk.

Then he showed her the pasted-up dummy copy he was working on, which would eventually be the next issue of the *Bridge*. "Things have to fit somehow, no matter how many stories or pictures go into it. There's just so much space and no more, so a good reporter learns to write his copy so that I can take out a whole paragraph, if I have to, without spoiling the sense of his story. Sometimes I have space left over. I keep a lot of jokes to fill in. We also have a gossip column and I can cut that or stretch it as I need to. When it's all finished, Mr. Woolrich, our adviser, looks it over and approves it before it goes to press. He doesn't bother us much. He trusts us."

Katherine was astonished. If this was all pretending, a game, it was certainly a fascinating one. Bob sounded like a real editor. He seemed much older and more responsible here.

The office and the work and the excitement of it stirred her in a way she would never have believed possible. It was a wonderful place. She wanted to be like that Audrey, suddenly; with a desk to work at and copy to write and a story to get. She'd even trade places with that boy, over there, who was doing a tedious and dull job of hunting names in what they called a "yearbook."

Why not? "I think it would be fun to work here," she told Bob. "I'd like to do it," and waited for him to say something.

He didn't seem to understand that she was offering to work for him. "It is fun. But it's hard, too. Stories have to come in on deadline and no nonsense. If some exciting news breaks, we have to scrap all the stories we've written and start all over again. When that happens, the staff members break their own dates, give up dances or parties and just stick to it until it's done."

"Why, of course." She would try again. "I wouldn't mind that. I shouldn't think anyone would."

"Are you going around with the Crowd?"

It was such a blunt question. It puzzled her. Was he trying to change the subject? "I guess I am," she said slowly. She looked at him; he was fiddling with the papers in one of his wire baskets, picking them up, acting as if he were reading them and then putting them down again. His face was turned away from her. He was behaving very strangely. "Yes, I suppose I am," she repeated. "They have been so friendly to me. Why?"

"I don't think you belong with them, that's why." He put down the papers and faced her. He was serious. "You don't seem like their kind of person—or you didn't, that first day we met. But if that's what you want, you aren't going to have any time for anything or anybody else but them. They'll see to that."

"Troy—"

"Troy's my sister—twin sister—and I don't even know what makes her tick any more. She's a little bit of Flip, a little bit of that Binky, a shadow of Chap and an echo of Jet—but she isn't herself. I don't know what she is."

"That doesn't make any sense to me," Katherine said. They were speaking low, so they couldn't be heard by the boy at the far corner of the room. "What does that have to do with me and—"

At that moment Marguerite Kelley walked into the room waving a sheet of paper. "Bob, have you got a minute? Hello, Katherine. Am I interrupting something?" She looked uncertainly at their troubled faces. "I've a poem here that a girl in my chemistry class wrote. It slipped out of her notebook this morning and I picked it up. She's too shy to bring it to you herself, but I think it's good. Take a look at it."

"Poems." He made a face, but he straightened up, moved away from Katherine and was once more the editor of the *Bridge*. "Okay, let's see it. Most poems I get are too silly to print." He ran a practiced eye rapidly down the paper and said, "Hey, this *is* good. Good and clever and funny. Just what I need. It's too long, though, and I'll have to cut out some of the third verse. It can be done if she's willing to change the line in the fourth verse so that it follows naturally. See? Look here, Marguerite, and you can explain it to her," and he and Marguerite crowded behind his desk, their heads bent over the paper while he made quick notes on the margin. "Ask her if she'd be willing to do that, will you?"

Katherine was completely out of it. She might as well have been a piece of unwanted furniture in the room, for all the attention either one of them paid to her. Their voices went on and on, Marguerite arguing that he was cutting out too much and that she didn't see how the poem could be cut without spoiling it, Bob saying that it had to be done because it was too long otherwise.

She stood there for a while and then slipped away quietly, without their noticing it. She didn't know, then, that what she was feeling was jealousy; she only knew that she disliked both Marguerite and Bob. Yes, and that girl reporter and the boy with the untidy hair and the fat artist—she disliked them all. Every one of them. They were doing interesting and exciting things; they had an importance about them; they were free to come and go in that wonderful, thrilling place where every week a newspaper was put together. And she was shut out!

No one had ever told her, she thought resentfully, that this activity outside of school classes would be such an exciting world of its own. Mr. Johns had tried to get her to join something or take an interest in something but, when he had said it, it was just words. She had thought the whole idea silly.

But it wasn't; it wasn't silly at all. They weren't playing games up there on the fourth floor. It was very real. Probably the Drama Club was like that and the actors who were taking part in the plays had that same dedicated feeling, taking part in something important. Actually she couldn't be sure about that and she didn't really care very much. It was that little, closed-off, dramatic office of the *Bridge* that she wanted. Her fingers itched for pencil and paper and a story to write.

"Run down and get an interview with the football coach, will you, Katherine?" . . . "That's a terrific story you wrote about the International Club, Katherine"—the words floated like a dream inside her head and the voice that was complimenting her was the voice of Bob Macdonald.

"Kit!"

Someone was *really* calling her. She came out of her dream to find herself on the main steps of the school with Jet hailing her from the front seat of his car. "Hi, Kit—where've you been? We've been looking all over for you. We're going over to my house. The folks are away for the day and we'll have the place to ourselves."

"I should go home and do some work," she said, but she let herself be pulled into the car. Troy and Chap and Flip were already there. Troy called something to her, from the back seat, but Katherine didn't hear.

"Hey—" It was Troy, tapping her on the shoulder. "Snap out of it. You look as if you were in a trance or something."

"Sleeping Beauty," said Chap.

She snapped out of it and looked at them then, and her heart warmed with the affectionate teasing they were giving her. They were her Crowd; they wanted her; she belonged with them. Those other people, on that fourth floor, didn't care whether she came or went or what she did. Katherine relaxed and smiled.

"I was in outer space, orbiting all by myself," she said.

"What was it like up there? Get tangled up with any stars?" Flip asked.

"It was cold. I almost froze to death. Then the nose cone came off and I got a piggy-back ride on a shooting star and it landed me right back here."

Flip giggled and Jet said, "Get her. What an imagination that kid has!"

They pulled up in front of Jet's house and climbed out just as Candy and George Yale sauntered up. While Jet was unlocking the door, Pedro braked his car to a halt and now the whole gang was there and having fun. Chap turned on the Hi-Fi and he and Troy picked out records to play. Binky, who was always hungry, produced a big sack of peanuts and handed them around; Jet and Pedro rolled up the living-room rug; Candy and George were on the sofa, talking; Red, without a date, was roaming around happily and getting in everyone's way; Toby was never three feet from Binky.

"Cut it out, Red, you clown. You're standing on a corner of the rug; we're trying to roll it up," objected Jet. "We want to dance."

"Oh, is that it? I thought maybe you were going to scrub the floor," kidded Red.

Katherine whispered to Flip while the two girls were shifting the coffee table out of the way, "Doesn't Red mind seeing Candy with George Yale?"

Flip shook her head and whispered back. "No. They never did really go for each other. Candy likes lots of compliments and Red would never give them to her, while old George is always telling her how beautiful she is. He's a drip, but"—she shrugged her shoulders—"if Candy wants him we'll have to put up with him."

"I think that's wonderful, the way you—I mean, we—always stick together," Katherine said. Once you were *in*, you were *in*; the Crowd didn't turn against you or reject you, no matter what you did. The idea made her feel proud of them and happy that she was one of them.

"Come on, Kit, let's dance." Jet took her hand.

"I can't. I don't know how," she objected.

"At your age?" George Yale guffawed. "Who ever heard of a girl your age not knowing how to dance?"

She felt the muscles of Jet's arm tighten, then relax. "If she doesn't know how to dance, that's her business," he said, clipping the words short. "Come on, Kit. I'll teach you. Now you just walk until you catch the rhythm of what I'm doing. Don't try to think about it; don't watch my feet or your feet; just let yourself follow me whenever you're ready. Walk until you get the beat."

It was surprisingly easy to learn. She did as Jet said and soon she stopped walking and began to catch on to what he meant by following him. It didn't go perfectly, of course; sometimes she stumbled, sometimes she went sideways when he wanted her to go forward but it was much easier than she had thought.

Everyone encouraged her. "Look, Kit—watch Chap and Troy. They're the best dancers and they're doing just what Jet was trying to teach you," Toby urged when Katherine sat down to rest for a moment. George came by just then and insisted he was a better teacher than Jet. He wasn't but she danced with him, anyway, because she knew he was trying to show her he was sorry he had laughed; he wanted to make up for his mistake and have them like him.

For nearly two hours they danced, or sat around and talked, or just listened to the music, ate Binky's peanuts and some potato chips Jet found in the kitchen. Nothing was said of any importance; almost everything was said for a laugh. In fact, Katherine realized—when someone happened to mention Marguerite Kelley—the Crowd didn't like anyone who was, in their opinion, too serious.

"She's in my gym class," Flip was complaining. "It's a special class for those of us who aren't supposed to have enough muscles for regular gym, so they give us modern dance. The rest of us just fool around with it but that Marguerite takes it so seriously. She goes swooping around and flopping on the floor—like this—" Flip got up and did a wild imitation. The contrast between her dead-pan, solemn face, so exactly like Marguerite's, and her arms and legs going in all directions, was so funny that Katherine laughed until her sides ached.

"That's nothing." Binky wiped her eyes and tried to stop

giggling. "Her mother and my mother are friends; they belong to the same church group and Mrs. Kelley and my mother are always baking cakes and stuff for church suppers. Then my mother comes home and says, 'Why can't you be like Marguerite? Why can't you be class secretary?'—or whatever it was Marguerite did last year. I get so sick of it."

"Somebody told me," George Yale offered, "that she's going to run for vice-president of the class this year."

"Now that's the job for me." Jet was stretched out, full-length, on the window seat. His house had a bay window just like the Normans'. "I'd like that. Vice-presidents are big shots but they never have to do any work. The president and the secretary and the treasurer—they all have jobs, but the vice-president just sits up on the stage at assemblies and looks important and doesn't do anything."

"You a class officer?" hooted Pedro.

"You think I can't, boy? You think I couldn't make it?"

George Yale broke in excitedly. "Sure you could, Jet! If you wanted it, we could swing the nomination and the election for you. You'd be surprised how many at school look up to you. I know they'd vote for you."

Jet looked thoughtful, but the rest were embarrassed at George's enthusiasm over what they considered to be just a joke.

"Well, let's break this up." Chap got up and stretched. "I've been promising my Dad for weeks that I'd mow the lawn and he's about ready to crack down on me. So I'd better get it done today."

Guiltily Katherine remembered that another paper was due for Miss Sunderman and she was glad when Pedro and Troy began rolling back the rugs and putting the room to rights.

7

She had forgotten all about Aunt Debra and that her aunt had forbidden her to see Jet, until he drove her up to the house. She was relieved to see that her aunt's car was not there; they could park and she could tell Jet what had happened.

"I know it's unfair," she explained. "But I can't invite you to the house any more. I don't know what to do. She's wrong, but it's her house and I have to do what she says."

Jet was angry. He hit the steering wheel, hard, with the flat of his palm. "Who does she think she is? You should have seen her at the hotel, ordering everyone around, telling everybody what to do, snooping into everything, and all the employees bowing and scraping to her. Yes, Miss Norman. No, Miss Norman. Whatever you say, Miss Norman." He was scowling. "Look, what she wants just isn't possible. She hasn't forbidden you to see Troy and the others, has she? It's not your fault if I'm there, too, when you go to see Troy. When you go out with the Crowd, it's not your fault that I'm part of it. When we come back home I'll always leave you off across the street, at the Macdonald house. What do you say?"

She didn't like it. It would be the first time in her life she had ever deceived anyone. Yet Aunt Debra was being unfair and to do what she asked would be to act unfairly, herself. Besides, Jet was right. Not to see him meant not seeing Troy and the others; it meant she would no longer be part of the Crowd. Not even Aunt Debra could ask that of her! "I guess you are right, Jet," she said reluctantly. She didn't feel romantic about Jet; she wasn't in the least bit in love with him; he wasn't important.

But the Crowd was, and so was belonging to it. For that she would deceive Aunt Debra.

For the next two months all of Katherine Norman's time, except for her classes at school and her studying at home and the routine work she did in the house, keeping strictly to the schedule, was spent with the Crowd. She went to the movies with them on Saturday nights; spent Sunday afternoons with them at the beach, where it was too cold to go in swimming but not too cold for a bonfire and a wienie roast; watched television programs at Pedro's house because his family had a separate TV room; danced at Jet's house because his mother didn't care if they scarred up the living-room floor; sat all together at football games and talked and laughed so much among themselves they didn't know, half the time, what was going on down on the field.

They knew that some of the students thought they were too rowdy and careless; others resented them because they were a clique; still others envied them . . . the Crowd didn't care. They were self-sufficient.

Katherine was proud of being one of them. Only, sometimes —just once in a while—something would happen that would make her wonder if all this carefree playing was what she really wanted. She studied hard and kept up her good grades only because she knew she could not bear to open her father's letters if she let him down; outside of that, nothing seemed to matter very much.

On the Saturday morning after she had visited the editorial offices of the *Bridge,* she had met Bob Macdonald outside her house. They were both waiting for the postman, again.

"What happened to you?" Bob asked, rather gruffly. "Why did you run out of the office the other day? I had to talk to Marguerite because we were on deadline for getting out the paper; and if that poem was to go in, it had to be settled then or not at all. When I looked up you were gone. I couldn't figure it out because you seemed so interested in the newspaper and all that we were doing."

For a moment all the fascination and the excitement she had felt in the *Bridge* office came back to her and she had that same ache to be a part of it. "I loved it," she said wistfully.

He shrugged. "Then I don't understand."

"You and Marguerite—you didn't even remember that I was there—you were so busy with the newspaper—" she stammered.

"Marguerite has nothing to do with the *Bridge*. She doesn't work for it. She's just a swell person and if she can help somebody, as she was helping me and the girl who wrote the poem, then she'll go out of her way to do it. You really should get to know her better. She doesn't have much of a sense of humor, so what? She'll knock herself out to help you."

"I don't need her help," Katherine flashed at him. "I'm quite all right, thank you."

"I know. When I missed you that day I looked out the window and I saw you getting into Jet's car. If that's what you want—"

"Now, listen, you two," drawled a voice behind them, "are you quarreling?" Mr. Bean was regarding them both with a shrewd glance. "You don't want to quarrel with a nice girl like Katherine, Bob. Are you mad because she gives me all her foreign stamps, instead of giving them to you?"

He meant to make them laugh and they both tried, because they liked him. But it was not genuine laughter and Katherine took her letter and went quickly into the house. "Thank you, Mr. Bean," was all she could manage to say.

All that day she couldn't get Bob and the *Bridge* out of her thoughts. She had a feeling something valuable had slipped out of her grasp.

Another time Aunt Debra said something that brought her up short, and opened her eyes to an aunt who was not just a tyrant but a very tired, very worried, very troubled woman with serious problems of her own.

For two months she and her aunt had lived together as polite strangers. The day after their quarrel Miss Norman had said, "I'm waiting for an apology, Katherine," and Katherine had answered in the same formal tone, "I am sorry if I was rude, Aunt Debra."

"Then we won't mention it again," her aunt had replied. Katherine knew she accepted the apology as a matter of form, and there were no more overtures toward friendship. Aunt Debra seemed relieved that there was nothing more expected from her.

This particular day, at breakfasttime, Aunt Debra's own worries broke through her usual restraint. She had no appetite. She sat crumbling some toast between her fingers, studying her coffee cup as if there might be some answers there. Finally she pushed her plate away. "I do wish," she burst out, "that Mr. Dale—our general manager—would tell me what he is up to. He is away in New York all the time and acting so mysteriously, having meetings with people. It leaves me with all the responsibility for the office. I don't mind that, but I do mind not knowing what's going on."

"It doesn't seem fair," agreed Katherine in her usual polite tone. She was startled, though. She had never seen her aunt so agitated. "You have to do so much more work. You've been going back to the hotel night after night and all day on Saturdays."

Her aunt made a pushing motion with her hand. "I don't mind it. What I do mind is the mystery. It starts all sorts of rumors flying around and that's bad for morale and bad for the hotel."

"What sort of rumors?"

"Oh, the usual sort of thing," impatiently. "That the hotel is going out of business. That there is going to be a shake-up of employees. The head clerk of the reception desk is sure that it is his job alone that is threatened. The captain in the dining room is positive that the Marlborough is going to eliminate our expensive dining room and substitute a coffee shop, and he'll be out of a job. They all come running to me for information and sympathy and I can't give them any. I do wish Mr. Dale would get back from New York, or that he'd write me and tell me what's true and what isn't true."

This was the longest speech Aunt Debra had made in weeks. Their usual conversations ran to "How is school? How is the office? Will you shell the peas for supper? Are you going back to the hotel this evening? Shall I leave the light on for you? The newspaperboy was here last night, collecting. I didn't have enough money for him, Aunt Debra."

It had been that sort of thing, so that Katherine was surprised and troubled at her aunt's outburst. It made her feel uncomfortable, knowing Aunt Debra had problems, too, and very serious ones.

"Why doesn't Mr. Dale say anything to you?" she ventured to ask.

"If I knew the answer to that," was Debra Norman's tart reply, "then I'd know the answer to everything. He has never behaved this way before; he has always confided in me." Then she brought her thoughts away from the hotel and herself and looked squarely and thoughtfully at Katherine. "I do hope you are considering your own future. Schoolbooks aren't enough, you know, unless they lead to something. Have you thought about what you want to be? About a profession or a career? You don't want to wait until you are in college to find out what your interests and aptitudes are; your father might not be able to afford college for you. I'd hate to think that you'd be in the same position I am, at my age; with no training except what I've learned for myself, and dependent now on the whim of an employer. I *always* wanted to write advertising for the hotel."

"You did?" This was an astounding revelation.

"Mr. Dale thought it was nonsense. He said he had trained experts to do that work and I should stick to my typewriter." She pushed herself away from the table and rose. "That's all past and gone; water under the bridge. But *you* should start thinking of a profession."

Katherine felt shy about speaking of something so secret to herself. "I thought perhaps I could write something someday. Or work on a newspaper." She kept her eyes lowered and she aimlessly pushed her scrambled eggs around on the plate in front of her, with her fork.

Her aunt was pinning on her apron. She snorted. "Wanting to write seems to run in our family. If you want to, then do something about it; don't just talk about it. Go see your teachers and ask them for advice." She went out to the kitchen and began running hot water into the dishpan. She called out, "Do hurry up! Stop making a mess with those scrambled eggs and eat them, or you'll be late."

Stung, Katherine retorted, "You didn't eat anything at all for breakfast."

"I wasn't hungry."

Katherine suddenly realized her aunt was eating too little and getting very thin. The homely face in the tall, angular body was growing gaunt and haggard.

That conversation made her thoughtful. What did she want to be? How should she go about picking out a profession and training herself for it? She remembered Mr. Johns's advice when she had started school that first day. He had talked to her of the importance of after-school activities; about how it would develop her as she learned to work with others. Perhaps these activities might also help her to choose a career. She hadn't thought of that.

All day long she worried about it, so it was a great relief when the telephone rang at seven that evening and Troy begged her to come over. "Flip's here and Binky's here and I've made a cake out of packaged mix and we're going to eat it all ourselves. Please come, Kit—it won't be any fun unless you're here."

It was a relief to go over and sit in Troy's bedroom and talk about nothing important and giggle over nothing in particular and eat chocolate cake and forget her problems. When the cake was gone, Troy got up and carefully locked the door, being as secretive about it as she could, listening at the door for any footsteps outside. Her face was full of daring and mischief; dramatically she put her finger to her lips and then pulled a package of cigarettes out of her dresser drawer.

"Troy!" Flip squealed. "Where did you get them?"

"Never you mind where I got them. My Dad won't miss one package out of his carton. Are we all game to try?"

"I am," Binky said promptly.

Flip reached out a hand for one. "Might as well try now as later. I'm old enough."

Katherine shook her head. "I can't. My father always let me do pretty much as I liked, but he did ask me not to smoke. He said when I was older I could, if I really wanted to, but not to do it now just because I think it's smart."

"Oh, don't spoil everything," Binky protested. "If we smoke, you have to."

"I don't," said Katherine stubbornly.

"You do, too," Flip argued. "That's our code. Do you think we're going to let you sit there and look disapproving? It will spoil the whole thing."

Troy settled matters. With a quick gesture she took back the cigarette still dangling from Flip's hand, threw it and the rest of the package onto the top shelf of her bookcase. She opened the door, wide. Her face was half-ashamed, half-defiant.

"That's that. Kit's right. I didn't really want to. Dad told me once that if I smoked I wasn't to do it secretly or behind locked doors; he'd rather I'd be open about it. Tonight was just a crazy idea of mine. I thought it would be a thrill. Don't pout, Binky; you should know Kit by now—once she makes up her mind she's as stubborn as a mule." Troy grinned. "That's what I like about Kit. You think she just gets along with everybody, nice and easygoing, but every once in a while you see she has a personality of her own."

They were all three looking at her, with a kind of odd appraisal, and Katherine blushed and quickly changed the subject. "What are we going to do Sunday afternoon? Jet said something about all of us meeting over at his house, but I don't know what we're going to do."

"Who cares?" The pout had gone from Binky's face and she stretched out flat on the bed. "We'll just play it by ear and see what happens. I hate making plans."

They all agreed. It was much better not to worry your head over the next day or the next Sunday—or the future.

Another two weeks went by in this aimless fashion. Once in a while Jet would get bored and then he would do rash and reckless things; the old game of seeing what they could take from—and return to—the Food Shop would start up again, and stop only when Jet was bored with it, too. Or he would drive his car too fast and force Pedro to race. Or he would start a feud with a particular teacher and bait him in class until the teacher's patience was almost exhausted. Then Jet would stop, just at the point of real danger, relax, and once again be good-natured.

"They're all such silly things," Katherine protested to him once. They were at the amusement park at the beach, standing at the rail, watching Troy and Chap and Candy and George Yale bump each other around the floor in the little electric carts which seemed to have minds of their own; backing up when Troy wanted to go forward, sidling along when Chap was trying to aim at Candy. "Why did you want to pick a quarrel with a teacher? You told me once that Mr. Murray was a pretty good guy, so what was the point of it?"

He just laughed. "I don't know, Kit. I really had old Murray on the run for a while; he couldn't keep any discipline in that class. After a while I had everybody doing it. Whenever he'd say anything we'd all yawn or sit and stare at him until he went crazy, but it wasn't anything he could actually bear down on us for." He took her arm. "Come on, let's go for the big one—we can meet them later."

The big one was the roller coaster. After the first dizzy, terrifying swoop downward, the rest of the ride was just a blur to her. She knew she was screaming and that Jet was laughing as they climbed and fell, shot madly around in circles and spun, tilting, around curves only to plunge at breakneck speed down to the bottom again. When it was all over and the car came to a stop and she stepped out, her legs were trembling.

Jet was relaxed and happy. "Come on—let's go up again," he urged.

"Never—never again," she gasped.

"Don't be chicken!"

She had recovered her breath and her legs had steadied. "I'm not chicken. I just don't like it, but I can see why *you* like it. It's crazy and wild and dangerous—and absolutely useless. It's the kind of challenge that has no reason to it."

He stopped and faced her. "What's the matter with you? If you want one of these onward-and-upward guys, full of noble enterprises and great deeds, you'd better get somebody else. Not me. You sound like that George Yale, who is always after me to run for vice-president."

It was significant of the way they all regarded George that he, alone, had no nickname. He still did not fit into the Crowd. He hero-worshiped Jet in a way that was embarrassing. Ever since the day the others had laughed at Jet for mentioning the vice-presidency, George had stoutly declared that Jet could win. He brought the subject up over and over again. They were all tired of it, though in some moods Jet could be flattered by the thought of winning an election.

Katherine and Jet patched up their quarrel. Another week went by.

Suddenly everything seemed to happen to her at once. Suddenly the aimless, drifting current she had been floating on turned into shoals and rapids.

It was a Wednesday. After her class in American history Miss Sunderman had asked, "Katherine Norman, will you remain for a few minutes? I want to speak to you."

Katherine wasn't worried. She had come to realize that under Miss Sunderman's snappishness was the brilliance of an excellent and fair teacher. She did wonder, however, what it was all about, when the rest were gone and Miss Sunderman picked up the latest report she had written and glanced over it.

"I read this last night," the teacher said. "It is very good. You have studied hard. More than that, it is exceptionally well written. You seem to have a flair, a talent, for making what could be a dull report into an exciting story. Have you thought of writing as a career?"

"I have thought about it. I'd like to work on a newspaper." Katherine was both pleased and astonished.

"Journalism? Well, I see no reason why we shouldn't talk to Mr. Johns, your counselor, and see if you can't take journalism next semester. You've done well and proved you can handle more work than the average student. Next semester, with all the special studying you've done now, you'll be up with the class in American history and I won't require so many additional reports from you."

"Thank you very much, Miss Sunderman. I'd like to take the class in journalism."

As Katherine was leaving, Miss Sunderman asked, as if the thought had just struck her, "Why not speak to Mr. Johns and to Bob Macdonald about doing some special work for the *Bridge?*"

"I told Bob Macdonald weeks ago that I'd like to work there but he wasn't the least bit interested. He pretended he didn't hear me." With her arms folded and her eyes flashing, Katherine looked the picture of indignation.

Miss Sunderman wasn't impressed. She sniffed. "Had he ever seen any of your work? No? Then what did you expect? He can't take on reporters, students who haven't shown any promise at all, just on their say-so. You have to prove what you can do, Katherine." Then she smiled. "Show him this paper and see what he says."

She went home in a daze. Should she show it to Bob? Risk his turning it down? The memory of the way he had ignored her to talk to Marguerite still rankled. Besides, he no longer liked her; he was disgusted that she spent all her time with the Crowd.

For a moment, outside her house, she was tempted to run across the street and see if Bob was home. The impulse was checked by the sight of something that frightened her—Aunt Debra's car sitting in the street when it was not even four o'clock in the afternoon. She ran up the stairs and let herself in with her key.

Her aunt was not downstairs. The house seemed too quiet; too deserted. It was frightening. Then, as she listened, she heard the sound of coughing and sneezing from upstairs.

"Aunt Debra?" Katherine hesitated outside her aunt's bedroom. "Is that you? Are you all right?"

The voice came weakly from behind the closed door. "I'm afraid I have picked up a cold or the flu. I'm so tired I came home early and went to bed. You aren't to worry; I shall be all right. A good night's sleep is all I need. Can you get your own dinner?"

"Of course I can, Aunt Debra. But isn't there anything I can do for you?"

"Nothing, thank you." There was another fit of coughing and then silence.

Katherine went slowly to her own room. It was impossible to think of Aunt Debra as ill; she had always seemed like an efficient machine that could never run down. Katherine thought that perhaps she should do something—call a doctor—but she couldn't take the responsibility on herself when Aunt Debra just wanted to be left alone.

She studied for an hour; she went downstairs to press a blouse.

That finished, she looked in the refrigerator and speculated about dinner. There were the remains of the pot roast from last night and there were vegetables of all kinds. She wrinkled her nose at the pot roast. Aunt Debra had a way of cooking it so that the meat was tender but absolutely without flavor or taste.

It was strange to have the kitchen all to herself. She thought: This one night I can have dinner exactly the way I like it.

She put on an apron, took the pot roast out and warmed it on top of the stove. In another saucepan she cooked carrot chunks until they were almost tender and then added them to the roast, along with a cupful of onions she had sautéed in a frying pan. Then, recklessly, she tossed a bay leaf, pepper, salt, thyme, oregano, a sprinkling of paprika and a squeeze of garlic juice into the simmering pot roast. The cover went on tightly and the flame was turned down low.

It felt wonderful to be really cooking again. This was the way she used to fuss and experiment with the dishes she had prepared for her father. He would say, "Katherine, you're a born cook; the pinch-of-this and the bit-of-that kind of cook." It almost always turned out wonderful.

She was about to put the onions away—large, red, Spanish ones—when she remembered the onion soup she used to make and how good it used to taste when she had a cold in her head.

So, while the pot roast simmered slowly on the stove, she cut the onions into very thin slices, cooked them in bacon fat until they changed color and became transparent. Then she sprinkled a little flour on them and stirred until the flour was slightly browned. A cup of the pot-roast juice, with water and a beef bouillon cube, was added to it. While it was cooking, she cut stale bread into cubes, rolled them in melted butter and garlic and toasted them in the oven to a crisp crustiness.

Half an hour later she knocked at Aunt Debra's bedroom door.

"Come in," came the hoarse croak. Debra Norman raised herself up by one elbow, turned on her night-table lamp and stared in astonishment at Katherine and the tray she was carrying. "For me?" she faltered.

"For you," Katherine said firmly. "It's onion soup and it is good for you."

Her aunt looked suspiciously at the tray, which held a covered bowl; a smaller bowl of grated cheese, another of toasted croutons; a teapot, cup and saucer and a flat glass dish of lemon slices and mint leaves. In one corner of the tray Katherine had dropped a geranium flower she had found in the back yard.

"You shouldn't have gone to all this trouble. I don't think I can eat anything." But Aunt Debra lifted the cover from the bowl and the sharp fragrance of the soup was too much for her. She lifted the spoon and tasted it. "Why, this is delicious! I didn't know we had canned onion soup in the house."

"I made it. It's not canned," Katherine said. Strange, but the sight of her aunt helpless, in bed, her voice weak and her long Norman nose all red, seemed to reverse their positions. It was Katherine who was giving the orders and her aunt who was dependent. "Now you eat it all and drink the hot tea; it's good for you, Aunt Debra. I'll just clean up this night stand for you." She swept all the used tissues into a wastebasket and put a fresh supply on it. "I'll get you a pitcher of water."

She found a second pillow and put it carefully behind her aunt's back so that the sick woman could sit up straighter, yet not disturb the tray on her knees.

When Katherine came back with the pitcher of water and a glass, Debra Norman had almost finished the soup. She was too weak to take more than small sips and she frequently put the spoon down to rest, but it was good and she was hungry and she had managed most of it. Now she was drinking the tea.

"You shouldn't have gone to all this trouble," she repeated. "I can't remember the last time anyone ever waited on me like this." Debra Norman was having trouble getting used to the idea; it was hard for her to thank Katherine, yet gratitude shone out of her weak and reddened eyes. She was resentful at being an invalid, yet Katherine had a strong impression that her aunt wanted her to stay and not leave her alone.

Katherine leaned over and squeezed the lemon into the tea. "It's the lemon that does you the most good, you know."

Aunt Debra wiped her nose roughly with a tissue, squinted up at her niece, took a sip of the tea and then sank back into the pillows. "Bless the child," she said in a voice Katherine had never heard before, "she talks as if she were a trained nurse and I were an infant. Where did you learn all of this, Katherine?"

"You know Daddy! He was always forgetting his raincoat and getting soaked in the rain and coming home with a cold. I used to make all kinds of things for him—orange-flower water and camomile tea and cool juices, not ice-cold ones. A doctor once told me not to give ice-cold liquids when someone had a cold."

"You took care of him? I hadn't realized that. I used to take care of him, too. He was younger than I, and when we were left without parents I had to nurse your father through colds, too." She smiled, Katherine smiled back at her and a link was born between the two of them. Then Aunt Debra went into a fit of coughing and Katherine quickly took the tray away.

"You'd better rest now. Perhaps I should go and let you sleep?" Katherine asked.

The coughing had passed and Aunt Debra's head was back resting on the pillow. She looked at her niece hesitatingly. "I'm not at all sleepy. I'm restless. I don't want you to catch my cold but I wonder if—if you couldn't bring your schoolwork here and work over by that desk. I won't disturb you, really."

She can't admit she's lonely, Katherine realized with a jolt of surprise. She's a lonely woman who doesn't know how to be friendly and hasn't thought it was important to be friendly. It could be that she's just sick tonight and is acting in a strange way, but I don't think so. I think the illness has broken down her defenses.

She brought back the American history books she was studying, her notebook and pen. The gooseneck lamp on her aunt's desk made a good light and, when she lifted the portable typewriter off the desk, there was ample room in which to work. "I have to write a paper," she said over her shoulder, "about the gold-rush days and how all the Americans coming out here for gold and settling down here to live brought California into the United States."

There was silence in the room for a long while as Katherine read and made notes and her aunt rested and watched her.

Then Katherine got up and stretched. "My back gets tired when I sit still so long," she explained.

Debra Norman said suddenly, "An ancestor of ours was in that gold rush. He was one of the early settlers of San Francisco."

"I didn't know that!" Katherine exclaimed.

"Oh, yes, we Normans are an old, old family here. The first Cyrus Norman came across country in a wagon train. They were headed for Oregon, to find lands and homes, but halfway there they heard the news of the finding of gold. Cyrus and the rest of the younger men in the train broke off from the others and headed for California. We still have some of his old letters, written to his sweetheart back in Illinois. Cyrus filed on a claim, but he couldn't find gold so he came to San Francisco instead. It was just a small town then." She stopped for breath and blew her nose.

"Should you be talking, Aunt Debra?"

"Do you want to hear this or don't you?" came the tart reply. When Katherine laughed, her aunt continued, "Well, Cyrus tried to start a grocery store because eggs were selling for a dollar apiece and all prices were sky-high. That failed, too. A rival burned his store to the ground. Finally Cyrus—your father is named after him—noticed that the pies at his boardinghouse were wonderful and he complimented the landlady who made them. She was a widow."

110

Aunt Debra settled back comfortably and Katherine leaned forward, all attention. My family, Katherine thought. Our family. Daddy never told me anything about them.

"Cyrus convinced the widow that if she would make the pies and cakes he'd start a restaurant and run it and they would go into partnership. It was a success from the beginning. He served good food and he helped cook the meals, but the pies and cakes were the specialties. Then he wrote his sweetheart to come out and join him, but she was having her problems; her parents were afraid to let her make such a dangerous voyage, overland or by sea. So Cyrus began to pay more and more attention to the widow. One day a ship came into harbor. Everyone rushed down to the docks to see whom the ship had brought and what its cargo was, and there on the dock whom should Cyrus find, among the passengers, but his sweetheart! That young girl, your great-great-grandmother, had run away from her home and taken ship all by herself to find the man she loved. She had guessed about the widow from Cyrus' letters and no widow was going to get her man."

"What a marvelous story!" Katherine said, a warm glow around her heart. "Did they get married? Did Cyrus Norman's restaurant go on being a success?"

"Yes—to both questions. San Francisco has always been famous for its fine eating places and I like to think that our ancestors helped start this tradition. Of course the restaurant passed out of the family; his son didn't like the business and became a doctor."

Katherine was deep in thought.

"Go back to your work, Katherine. I'll try to rest awhile."

"Aunt Debra," Katherine said slowly, "I have an idea. Why shouldn't I write the story of Cyrus Norman and his adventures, instead of writing a dull account of how men came out for the gold rush and how they settled down here? Our ancestor's story is the story of the settlers, the real ones, who stayed on to build up this state."

"Don't make the story too pretty, Katherine," her aunt warned. "From Cyrus' letters those were brutal times as well as good times. A lot of injustices took place. Men were murdered for their claims. A Mexican friend of Cyrus was defrauded of his land by an unscrupulous land grabber and a clever lawyer."

"I'll put all that in the story," Katherine agreed.

By nine-thirty she was finished. Debra Norman had napped, awakened, dozed off again. She was snoring loudly now as Katherine softly tiptoed to the bed, turned off the light and went to her own room.

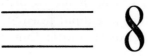 8

The next morning Aunt Debra was no better; if anything, she was worse. Katherine took one look at her and decided to stay home from school—and her aunt protested feebly.

"You shouldn't."

"I'm going to. And don't you argue with me." Where in the world, Katherine thought in amazement, had she found the courage to talk to her aunt like that? It didn't even take courage; she was enjoying it.

She fixed orange juice, more hot tea, and buttered toast that was soft in the middle—in case her aunt's throat was sore. A small omelet, such as she had been taught to make in France, was a tempting golden roll on the plate she offered her aunt.

Debra Norman tasted it, then croaked hoarsely. "I had no idea you were such a cook! Maybe you take after your ancestor, Cyrus Norman." She ate as much as she could but hardly touched the toast and finally she had to say, "I think you'd better call Dr. Jenniver. His number is in that green address book on my desk."

While Katherine was hunting for it she heard a strange, harsh sound from the bed behind her; but when she whirled around, it was to find that that strange sound was her aunt laughing. "I was just thinking," Aunt Debra explained, "that maybe Cyrus' widow burned a pie now and then, just as you did the waffle. What if he had decided she couldn't cook—just the way I thought you couldn't?"

Then both niece and aunt burst out laughing and a great weight of misunderstanding rolled away from between them.

Katherine well understood that this was as close to an apology as Aunt Debra could ever come.

The doctor approved of Katherine's staying home to play nurse. "Not that Miss Norman needs much attention; just rest, and aspirin and fruit juices. Encourage her to eat a little dinner this evening. She seems to be quite run down. Too much work probably."

Katherine was quiet as she moved about the house, but her success with the cooking had gone to her head. She was bold enough to want to make all kinds of changes. She filled vases with flowers from the hydrangea bush outside the porch; she found wood in the basement and arranged it in the living-room fireplace, all ready for a touch of a match. She rearranged the smaller pieces of furniture, to break the stiff, formal discomfort of the living room and make it more comfortable.

All day Aunt Debra napped and dozed and read a little. She didn't feel like talking.

Troy came to the door after school but Katherine whispered to her, "I can't come out. I'm being nurse for Aunt Debra. She has a bad cold."

"Oh, you poor kid," Troy sympathized as she took her leave.

Behind the closed door Katherine stood stock-still, thinking. *Poor kid*. She was nothing of the sort; she was lucky. In one night and one day she had discovered the human being in Aunt Debra, the warmth that lay beneath that cold manner, the priceless knowledge that she was needed and wanted by her aunt.

Not an hour after Troy had left there was another knock on the door and it was Bob Macdonald, a copy of that week's issue of the *Bridge* under his arm, a chocolate bar in one hand and a comic book in the other.

"Troy told me Aunt Debra was sick and you were looking after her. The chocolate is for you, to keep up your strength," he said, "and the *Bridge* to improve your mind. The comic book is for Aunt Debra."

"A comic book?"

"She'll understand. When we were kids she always used to invite Troy and me over for Sunday breakfast so Dad and Mom could have some peace in the house, and then she'd read the Sunday funny papers to us. She used to get as big a kick out of them as we did. So maybe she'll get a laugh out of this, now."

Katherine took it dubiously, but she thanked him anyway.

"Now is there anything I can do for you?" he asked.

She thought for a moment. "There is something, if you wouldn't mind, Bob. I telephoned the school and explained about my absence, but I may not be able to go tomorrow either. Would you take a short composition I wrote to Miss Mailer? And this other report to Miss Sunderman? If I do that they will know I'm keeping up with the assignments."

"Sure. Glad to." His eye was caught by the title of the two sheets of paper she had clipped together for Miss Sunderman. "What's this? 'Pies and a Pioneer.' That's a catchy title. What's it all about?"

"Nothing. Just a story about old San Francisco and the gold-rush days."

He shuffled the papers together so they wouldn't wrinkle. There was an awkward silence between them as they stood in the dimly lit hallway; a silence because this was the first time in weeks they had been alone together and there seemed to be so much they both wanted to say and couldn't. She broke it by asking, timidly, "Would you like to come in and stay awhile? I made some cookies, and there's lemonade—"

"Thanks. I'd like to. I'm starving, as usual." He grinned.

They were moving toward the dining room when the telephone on the hall stand shrilled. She leaped to answer it before it could awaken Aunt Debra.

"Who? Oh, Jet. Hi. No, I'm all right; it's my aunt who's sick. Yes, I know I promised for tonight but I can't come. Tomorrow? I'm not sure. She may be better and she may not be. Who is that laughing? I can hear someone laughing. Oh, I see. Candy and Binky and Red are with you. Tell them hello for me. Your book? What book? No, I don't have it. Maybe you left it in the car or at Troy's—"

She heard a sound and looked up just in time to see Bob going out the door, closing it behind him. She was so stunned she hardly knew what she was saying to Jet and she cut him off short, replacing the telephone receiver.

Why had Bob gone like that? Yet she knew. That telephone conversation with Jet, so casual, really, must have sounded so intimate that Bob had felt as much in the way as she had felt that day in the *Bridge* office when he and Marguerite had their heads together over the poem.

She was so frustrated she could have cried, but Aunt Debra was calling from upstairs. Katherine arranged her face so that she could smile when she walked into the bedroom.

"How are you feeling?" she asked.

"Much better. I want to get up. I hate being an invalid. This bed is uncomfortable." Some of her testy manner had returned, but this time Katherine wasn't put off by it. "If you'll hand me my bathrobe, I'll go sit in the living room for a while and watch television."

Aunt Debra never even touched the television dial. When she came slowly downstairs and into the living room, she was too astonished to talk. Katherine ran on ahead, lit the fire and pulled a big upholstered chair in front of it. She made her sit sit down with her feet on the ottoman.

"Well, you *are* full of surprises. That fire does feel good." She sank back; straightened up to peer suspiciously at the fireplace. "Is it smoking? It does, you know. That's why I never use it. I won't have smoke ruin my curtains."

"It's not smoking a bit. I pushed the wood far to the back. Now you just relax and look at your present from Bob Macdonald."

Aunt Debra took the comic book, turned it over front and back in her hands, stared at it, held it up. "What's this? Of all the crazy things—that rascal! How do you suppose he ever remembered that *The Punkin Kids* was the one and only comic strip I ever really liked? I used to read all the rest of them to Troy and Bob and most of them were so downright silly that it was a chore, but the Punkin Kids were funny." She chuckled deep in her throat, then gave Katherine a belligerent glare. "I suppose you think it's ridiculous for a woman my age to read a comic book. I suppose it makes you feel superior and intelligent."

For just a second, temper flamed heat into Katherine's cheeks. The sight of her aunt's tight, pulled-in mouth checked her. That mouth was too tight, as if to stop it from trembling. Instinct prompted Katherine to do the right thing. She dropped to her knees by the side of the ottoman and put her head in her aunt's lap.

"Read it out loud to me, will you, Aunt Debra? I've never heard any American comics and I've always wanted to."

Pages rustled over her head. She didn't dare look up. There was the sound of her aunt clearing her throat; then came words, slow and awkward at first, stumbling, then smoothing out and Katherine caught the echo in them of a younger Aunt Debra who had once gathered her neighbor children around her knees to read to them on a Sunday morning. "Now, let's see— the Punkin Kids are at the seashore and Nella and Bobby are building a great big sand castle and they are both stretched out flat on the sand and in back of Bobby a little crab is inching his claws along toward Bobby's big toe and Nella says to Bobby (you know how *she* talks—so big and important for such a little girl), 'We are in the hands of Fortune, Bobby; in the claws of Fate; and then the little crab suddenly—'"

A hand dropped in an absent-minded way on her head, and Katherine breathed a sigh of deep, happy content. The foolish little story went on.

By the next morning Aunt Debra was well enough and she insisted Katherine go to school; but as soon as her last class was over, she rushed home. To her relief her aunt was up and about. Her nose was still red but she was her old, vigorous self.

"You get to your books," she commanded. "You've taken off enough time, nursing me. I'm going to give the kitchen a good, thorough cleaning. I called the hotel and Mr. Dale is back, thank goodness, so that's one worry off my mind. The office isn't being neglected."

When Katherine went to her room and her desk, she found the portable there.

"Aunt Debra," she called over the staircase, "shall I put your typewriter back in your room? Where do you want it?"

"I can give you a present, can't I?" came the cross answer from below. "I watched you last night, scribbling away. It's time you learned to use a typewriter and I'm going to teach you how."

"Oh, thank you!"

"Nonsense."

It wasn't nonsense and they both knew it. Katherine went back into her room and touched the typewriter with excited, reverent fingers. She was going to learn to use it and her aunt was going to teach her how.

The telephone rang and rang. It was Troy and then Binky and then Jet, but the call that came during their dinner was not for Katherine. Aunt Debra came back from the hall with shining eyes. "That was Mr. Dale, himself, and he's coming all the way out here this evening to call on me. That just shows you how kind he is and how much he appreciates all the work I've done for him while he's been away." She picked up her napkin. "He lives clear across town. Probably it's not so much to see me as that he needs some information. I suppose he can't remember where the last tax statement is filed, or maybe he needs some phone number."

"When he comes, shall I serve coffee or tea and some of those cookies I made?"

"Oh, no." Aunt Debra had on her office look. "I never mix social life with business. It just isn't done."

When the doorbell rang that evening Katherine was introduced to the plump, unhappy-looking, harassed man who was Mr. Dale. She excused herself and left her aunt and employer alone together, behind the closed door of the living room. Just the same, as she ironed a dress and a skirt in the kitchen, she could hear the rise and fall of voices, going on and on. It seemed to Katherine that, finally, it was only Mr. Dale, and her aunt was not speaking at all, not saying a word.

Katherine heard the living-room door open, the short murmur of voices, then the front door close behind Mr. Dale. In a few minutes she went into the living room, carrying her freshly ironed dress over her arm.

"I didn't put the ironing board away, Aunt Debra. I thought perhaps you—"

Something was wrong. Something was terribly wrong.

Her aunt was sitting absolutely still in her chair, not proud and stiff-backed, the way she always sat, but hunched over with her shoulders slumped and her head bowed.

"Aunt Debra! What's wrong? Are you ill again?"

"I'm not ill," came the slow, tired voice. "I've just been fired. After twenty years! Mr. Dale says the hotel was sold to new people. That's what he was doing when he was back East on all those visits—talking to the new owners. He never said a word to me. Now he says the new owners are transferring employees of their own, from a hotel in New York which they are abandoning, and bringing them to the Marlborough. Making a clean sweep of all of us! Putting in all those new people from New York."

"That's mean! It's unfair and cruel," Katherine cried.

"Mr. Dale softened the blow as much as possible by coming here instead of telling me in the office, where I'd have to face the others. It's hard on everyone, but I've been a sort of queen bee there so long that it would be more difficult for me."

"Is it the money, Aunt Debra? Will you be poor without the salary?" Katherine couldn't stand the change in her aunt.

Perversely, just then, she longed to have her aunt snap at her, scold her, tyrannize over her—anything but sit there, beaten and defeated.

"No. It's not the money. I have some saved. And they're giving me four months' salary, instead of a notice, because they want the change to take place immediately. I'm not to go back—not tomorrow or any other time! After twenty years. That office has been my life and I'm not even to set foot in it again."

Katherine understood. She had seen Debra Norman at the Marlborough, where she was so needed, so wanted, so indispensable, so important, with all kinds of employees coming to her for help and advice and orders. To give that up was more than just being fired from a job.

I must pretend not to notice. I must act as if I don't see her weakness.

She walked over and turned on a floor lamp, flooding the room with light. She poked at the dying fire, making it flare up again. Debra Norman blinked and shielded her eyes, but Katherine ignored the signs of tears. "There are lots of other offices and interesting jobs in a city like San Francisco," Katherine said, making her voice hard and unsentimental. "You'll find something a lot better than you had. We Normans are fighters. *You've* taught me that. You are just like old Cyrus Norman. He tried to find gold and couldn't, but he wasn't discouraged. He came to San Francisco and started a grocery store and it was burned down. Another man might have quit then, but not our ancestor. He found those pies and went into the restaurant business. I'm not worried about you, either."

It was having its effect. The tall figure in the chair had straightened up a little, but not quite enough. One hand was still in front of her face and the other trembled on the arm of the chair.

"Let's not think about it until tomorrow," Katherine went on, unrelenting. "I hate to be selfish, but would you start me on the typewriter tonight? I need to learn it so much and you're the only one who can teach me. Please, Aunt Debra—if I bring it down here, couldn't you give me a lesson?"

"Not right now, child."

"Oh, please! You promised."

Aunt Debra sighed and leaned back. "Very well, if you insist. Bring it down here. Get newspapers and spread them thickly on that table so the machine won't mar it. There's lots of yellow copy paper in the right-hand drawer of my desk; you can practice on that." A faint tinge of briskness was back in her voice as she gave her orders. "Tomorrow I'll buy you a self-teaching book so that you can practice from it."

Katherine rushed out in a flurry of activity. In a matter of minutes she was downstairs with the typewriter and paper, to find her aunt drawing a large-scale picture of the keyboard on a sheet of heavy paper, making circles on it for all the keys and lettering each of them.

Katherine felt her heart bound in admiration. Give Debra Norman something to do and all of her tough, pugnacious spirit was back again.

"You sit right there"—Aunt Debra placed Katherine in the chair in front of the table and typewriter—"and don't you ever, ever look at the machine. Keep your eyes on this drawing I've made and feel for the right keys. The worst thing in the world is to look at the typewriter. If you do, your fingers will never learn their right places automatically." She stood over her niece and placed her two hands so that the little finger of one rested lightly on the "A" and the little finger of the other was on the semicolon. "Now you must learn always to keep your hands in that position and reach the other keys without moving your hands around."

For half an hour Katherine practiced. It was hard. She made mistakes and Aunt Debra was a severe taskmaster, scolding her every time her head swiveled to look at the typewriter.

Yet Debra Norman had an incredible patience, a splendid way of teaching. No matter how many mistakes she made, her aunt would not permit discouragement. "Try again," she would say. "Paper's cheap. Keep going. The position of the keys on that drawing I made is the same as on the typewriter; look at the drawing and train your fingers to reach the right ones. Arch your fingers. Don't drop your wrists. You're doing fine."

Now is the time for all good men to come to the aid of the party. Katherine wrote it, "Nie us rhe tone to—" and all sorts of other weird combinations, but she persevered and by bedtime the sentence was almost perfect.

While they walked up the stairs together, Katherine knew quite well that her aunt would shed a few tears into her pillow that night; but she also had the good feeling that Debra Norman would be very much her own strong self by the morning. As they separated to go to their bedrooms she felt a hand pat her back, and her aunt said, "You are quite a person, Katherine. I'm sorry I didn't become acquainted with you before."

Now what did she mean by that? A *person?*

Did it have something to do with the letdown she experienced the next afternoon she spent with the Crowd? Her aunt was off job hunting and Katherine had joined the others at Jet's house. The scene was the same as it had been so many times: the rug was rolled up, the music was playing, some were dancing and others were in twos and threes talking. Yet she couldn't rouse herself and just have fun. It all seemed so trivial and unimportant.

Winning a smile from Aunt Debra had been a thrill. Here everyone smiled for no particular reason at all.

"What's the matter, Kit? You've been sitting there looking as solemn as an owl. A redheaded owl," Troy kidded her.

"I don't know what's the matter; but if I hear Binky squeal once more I think I'll squeal, too, or scream. Pedro and Flip always have to show off when they dance and George Yale follows Jet around—everybody does the same thing over and over again."

"You're in a mood." Troy fussed with her belt. "I know that

mood. I get it sometimes, too—when I feel we're all just a bunch of sheep baaing around each other in circles. But you'll snap out of it."

She didn't snap out of it. Every time she saw them it was worse. She began to avoid them, making the excuse that Aunt Debra needed her—which wasn't entirely an excuse. Going the rounds of the employment agencies day after day was not easy for a woman of Debra Norman's age and pride. She came home tired, sometimes out of temper, sometimes hurt; but whatever the reason, just the fact that Katherine was there, that a fire was burning on the hearth and a cup of hot coffee was ready, seemed to lift her spirits enormously.

"You'd think, with my background and experience," she'd say, sitting down on the sofa and letting Katherine take her hat off, "that it would be easy for me to step into a new secretarial job. No, sir—all the agencies want are young nincompoops who don't know anything. They put it tactfully but I'm no fool. They think I'm too old to start in something new. Well, I'm not looking forward to it myself, but I can do it if I get the chance."

Teaching Katherine in the evenings restored her faith in herself somewhat. Sometimes, when Katherine was a little discouraged over her progress, Aunt Debra would sit down at the typewriter and rattle off a couple of pages. Her fingers moved like lightning, with trip-hammer strokes that never made a mistake. "There!" she would say with satisfaction. "And they say I'm too old! You keep up this practicing and you'll be typing just as fast, one of these days."

9

At lunch time on Friday, Jet was in a scowling mood.

"Why did you turn me down last night, when I called you?" he asked Kit before she could even say hello or squeeze her way into the booth at the Food Shop. "What's this business of practicing typewriting?"

"Aunt Debra's teaching me. It's fun. I can write 'the quick brown fox' without making a single mistake now," she said.

"Fun? You kidding? Sometimes I just don't understand you; I really don't. What's fun about that? It's work. You know, Kit, most of the time you're like one of us, but then you pull a stunt like this and I don't know which side of the fence you're on. You want to be another Marguerite Kelley? Maybe you'd rather eat with her and Bob Macdonald. You'll find them over in the cafeteria." He turned his back.

She started to get up. "Don't you ever speak to me like that, Jet Smith. I'll eat where I please and I'll do whatever I please. You told me once you liked me because I got excited about things . . . well, I'm excited about a typewriter and if you don't like it—"

Chap had come up behind her and now he pushed her back down into the booth. "Stop it, you two. Apologize, Jet. Come on."

Katherine saw then why Troy liked Chap so much. When he wanted to, he had will power. His tone left Jet no chance to refuse or even to sulk. Jet's black eyebrows drew together for a second; then his whole face lightened in the charming, magnetic smile that transformed him.

"I'm sorry, Kit. Honestly. I was just upset because you

weren't with us last night. Forget it, will you? We're all going to the football game this afternoon, together. Did you bring a warm coat? It's going to be a foggy, damp afternoon."

"I have two sweaters and my jacket," Binky announced. "I'll lend you one of my sweaters, Kit, if you forgot about the game."

The storm was over. They all relaxed. Chap had a deck of cards and, while they waited for their orders, he began to build a house out of them. The house grew into a tower, high and higher. All of them, Katherine included, leaned forward to watch it.

"Don't blow on it," he begged. "It will fall down."

"Make it a skyscraper. A big one," Troy insisted.

He added three more cards, placing them so very carefully. Pedro's hand slid slowly under the table and he jiggled it slightly.

"Stop that," Chap commanded.

"No," Jet said, "we'll make it a bet. Each one can rock the table—just a little—and we'll bet on which one of us makes it fall down. Okay, Chap?"

"Okay."

"Then hands on the table, flat down. Nobody can jiggle with the knees, just the pressure of one hand. And only one push to a person. Ready? You're first, Pedro."

The cards teetered but didn't fall; nor did they for George, or Flip, or Red. It was Jet's strength and sudden thrust of flat hand and flat wrist that brought them tumbling down all over the table.

"The champion and the winner!" crowed George Yale, holding Jet's right hand up in the air.

They all applauded.

Success went to George's head. "The winner and the next vice-president of the senior class—I give you Jet Smith, ladies and gentlemen."

They all groaned. "*That* again, George?" Troy muttered.

Jet's little triumph had exhilarated him. Katherine knew and dreaded that mood in him, when he jumped from one crazy thing to another. He teased the waitress until she mixed up all their sandwiches and gave them to the wrong persons. He plagued Binky because she was left-handed, and jogged her elbow every time she took a bite. He challenged Pedro to a race at the beach the next Sunday. In this mood nothing satisfied him. He had to go on and on finding new outlets for his restlessness.

It was time to leave. The lunch hour was almost up. They moved in a straggling group to the cash-register counter to pay their bills. The Food Shop was deserted, except for them. The waitress was in the kitchen and even Mr. Coggins, who always presided over the cash register, was leaning over the front window, arranging a new display.

While his back was to them, Pedro took a paper napkin and put it in his breast pocket as if it were a handkerchief. Katherine saw Jet's eyes dart all around, looking for something. He spotted the dish of paper-wrapped chocolates, with the sign Two for Five Cents, beside the register. Scooping up a handful, he tossed two to Katherine. "Catch!" he whispered.

She let them fall at her feet. She stared at them and then at Jet. All the others had come to a halt and were watching them uneasily.

"Put those back, Jet," Katherine said in a fierce whisper. "Paper napkins are bad enough but this is something else. Put those back."

"What's the matter? Do you think I didn't mean to pay for them?"

"Then why are you whispering about it?" Katherine asked.

The proprietor of the Food Shop was coming toward them and Jet raised his voice. "Mr. Coggins, I just took six chocolates out of this tray. Add them to my bill, will you?" It was said with unnecessary loudness and swagger.

Katherine heard Troy and Chap and Flip let out a deep breath of relief. Once again, danger had been averted; once again, Jet was all right in their eyes. But not in hers. They could be as blind as they wanted to be. She was sure he had meant to take the chocolates without paying for them.

Even if he hadn't—now she knew what Aunt Debra had meant by her warning. The Marlborough had been quick to believe him capable of stealing a wallet because he had thought it smart to take hotel stationery; his actions came too close to the border line for Katherine to ever trust him again.

She paid her bill and walked out with Candy and George. At the foot of the main entrance to the school, Jet was waiting for her.

"Are you mad at me?" he asked. The others were listening.

"I don't want to ever see you again or talk to you again. You think you do such smart and clever and brave things and I think they're just plain stupid. What's so wonderful about taking things from Mr. Coggins? He isn't rich and it's not fair that you should—"

"Steal from him?" As usual, it was George who put his foot in it and said the unforgivable word. "Are you calling Jet a thief?"

The question—the word—her unspoken answer—hung between them. Silently the group parted and let Katherine walk through and up the steps alone.

The rest of her afternoon was a daze, full of feelings of shock at what she had done, relief at what she had done and fear of what was to come. Flip hinted at it when she passed her in the hallway without saying a single word. In their Lit class Troy stared straight at the teacher and never once looked around; when the second class was over, Troy was out of her seat in a flash, almost running out the door.

It was strange to walk out of school and find no one waiting for her. Katherine had picked up her copy of that week's issue of the *Bridge* and she had it tucked under her arm. Where should she go? Then she remembered the football game. She walked to the field and joined the pushing throng of students making their way into the grandstand. No one spoke to her; she spoke to no one. The Crowd had been so completely her life that she had made no other friends at school.

The place was crowded; she was almost the last student in, so she took the first empty seat she could find.

Not until she sat down did she realize she was directly in front of Jet—with Chap and Troy on one side of him, and on the other side all the rest. Never had she felt so embarrassed. She knew they were all looking at her, because they had been laughing and talking and now they were silent.

"Look who's here." That was Candy's voice. "I wonder if she wants us to leave. Maybe we're contaminating the air for her."

"Maybe she's here to see nobody steals the football." That foolish kind of laugh could only have come from George Yale.

"Cut it out" . . . "Leave her alone" . . . Jet and Troy had spoken at exactly the same time, in exactly the same tone of voice.

Katherine didn't look around. Her cheeks were hot and she clenched her hands in her lap. It was going to be worse than she had thought. The Crowd was furious with her; Candy and George and perhaps Flip would do their best to torment her, and the rest would cut her dead. Of all of them it was Troy's friendship which mattered the most, and the cold way Troy had said "Leave her alone" hurt worse than anything else.

A whistle blew and blue and gold figures fought against green and white down on the field below, but Katherine could barely see them for the tears in her eyes.

Not even when she had come to Golden Gate High School, a perfect stranger, had she felt so completely alone. She hadn't known then what it was like to be accepted, to be chosen as part of a group. It was awful to be rejected by them now. Would it be possible, with everybody standing up and yelling and watching the game, to slip past the six people on her left and get to the aisle and leave?

What had she told Aunt Debra? We Normans are fighters.

Her chin came up. Except for the red hair, there had never been any resemblance between Debra Norman's face and Katherine's soft, creamy-white oval face; but at that moment anyone would have known they were related. There was that same pugnacious, fearless, touch-me-not look.

At the half, when everyone settled back more or less quietly in their seats and the voices of Jet and Candy and the others were audible again behind her, she remembered the *Bridge* under her arm. She unrolled it and forced herself to concentrate on every single word of it. If anyone spoke to her or of her she wouldn't listen. Just the same, all through the front page, she was conscious of Jet right behind her and of the way he crossed his legs so that the toe of one shoe just touched the back of her shoulder.

Then she turned the page and forgot all about them, the game and everything else.

Right in the middle of the second page, in bold black type, was the title "Pies and a Pioneer"! And underneath it was her own by-line—Katherine Norman.

She clutched the paper hard and bent her head to read it more carefully. Yes, it was her story, every single word of it; the one she had asked Bob to give to Miss Sunderman. Katherine felt something brush her shoulder and the back of her neck; she looked around just in time to see Jet move away. But he had seen the story and her name—that was what he had leaned over to see. For just a second their eyes locked and she saw an odd expression in his, as if she had done something too strange to be believed.

She couldn't be sure because he immediately began talking loudly to Pedro, engaging him in a bantering argument. She paid no more attention to him; she was too excited about her story and she read and reread it, feeling a choking sense of excitement.

The minute she arrived home she telephoned the Macdonald house.

"Mrs. Macdonald, this is Katherine Norman. Is Bob there? May I speak to him?"

The pleasant voice was unhurried. "Katherine? Yes, dear, Bob's just home from the game and he's out in the garage with our youngest little demon, trying to keep him from blowing himself up with some chemicals. I'll call him."

Bob must have run from the garage; he was panting. "Hi! How's the famous Nellie Bly of Golden Gate High School? You don't know who Nellie Bly was? What kind of newspaper-woman are you? She was the first big-time woman reporter in the United States."

"Oh, Bob, I'm so thrilled and I do want to thank you. You never said a word about it and neither did Miss Sunderman."

"I wanted to surprise you," he said. "I remember the kick I got, the first time I ever had anything printed in the *Bridge* with my own name on it. There's nothing like it in the world."

She sighed happily. Bob understood. She sat down on the rug, her back against the wall, and made herself comfortable. The telephone receiver in her hand was a magical instrument. "I know what you mean. I feel as if I've done something really big for the first time in my life."

"It doesn't have to be the last time either. I'd like to have you do more stories like that for the paper. Not just history, but all kinds of feature stories. I didn't have any right to read your paper but I got so curious about that title I couldn't resist."

"What is a feature story?" she asked.

"It's not the same," he answered, "as straight reporting. Take the football game today. A reporter would write about the game itself: who won, by how much, where it was played and when, how many touchdowns and so on. But we might run a feature article, an interview with the coach on what he thought about our chances of winning. Sometimes a feature article can be serious, about the history of the school or some new course the school is offering or a teacher everybody likes. Or it can be funny—like 'Why Do Boys Like Girls?' or something like that."

"Or 'Why Do Girls Like Boys?' " she laughed. "I wouldn't know. Pick something easier for me."

"Okay, but you'll have to think up most of your ideas yourself. Keep your eyes and ears open around school; move about and get to know people. Circulate. You'll pick up stories and ideas all over the place," he said.

Bleakness settled around her heart where there had been that warm glow. Whom did she know in school? Only the Crowd. She had isolated herself from the rest of the students and didn't know anything about them, not even their names. "I'll try, Bob." Subdued, she said it quietly.

"Good girl. Will you have the time? I'd like to count on you for the next issue—no, that one is full. The next after that? Next issue is the Thanksgiving one—we'll soon have to be thinking of something for Christmas."

He said that "we" so confidently that she felt she couldn't let him down. "I'll have time, Bob. Honest. I'll bring you a couple of stories and you can choose which one you want." She would have liked to tell him she had broken with the Crowd, but he might ask why and she didn't want to tell him that. She had broken the code of loyalty that bound the Crowd; she had found it a false loyalty but she still wasn't going to gossip about them.

How was she going to go about making friends? It had been Troy who had picked her that first day at school, and so she had had to make no effort at all. Now she was alone, standing on her own two feet, and it was up to her to make the first moves.

Those students who didn't like the Crowd thought she had snubbed them before and weren't anxious to be friends now; those who admired Jet and Troy and Chap and the others, and thought them a special clique to be envied, thought there was something suspicious now that she was no longer one of that group. Or at least this was what Katherine imagined.

By the end of the week she took herself firmly in hand. It was Aunt Debra's example that did it—just watching her tall, bony figure, neat in coat and hat and immaculate gloves, with shoes shined to a high brown polish, bravely setting out every morning on a round of coldly uninterested employment agencies and prospective employers. If she could do that, Katherine could make a bigger effort at school.

That noon she marched into the cafeteria and sat down beside two strange girls, but this time she didn't prop a book up and read while she ate.

"Hello," she said to both of them, "this meat loaf looks good. How's your creamed chicken?" Inside she was groaning. Wasn't that bright, sparkling conversation she was making! Wouldn't Flip have laughed at her!

What was wrong with her? In Europe she had never been at a loss when it came to conversation. Even that first day at Golden Gate, when she had felt so strange, she hadn't been *afraid* to speak to anyone. Had she become a nothing without the Crowd?

Neither of the two girls had said anything, so she tried again. Turning to the brown-haired, brown-eyed girl, she said, "Haven't I seen you at school assemblies, singing German and French songs?"

A sudden smile blossomed and the brown eyes gleamed. "Yes. Did you like them? Which one did you like best?"

Frantically Katherine searched her memory. On that particular day Jet had sat next to her and made whispered comments all through the singing. She hadn't paid much attention. Then, suddenly, she remembered the name of one. "I liked that 'Las Mañanitas'—"

Both girls laughed. "That wasn't French or German. That was Mexican. How come a girl like you, who has lived abroad, wouldn't know that?"

"How do you know I've lived abroad?" Katherine relaxed. The atmosphere around the table had become friendly.

"Mr. Johns told me. He's my counselor, too, and he suggested I might talk to you about France and Germany and those countries because I may be going to study there next year. I didn't, since you never came into the cafeteria until this week and you were always with a bunch of kids after school."

"I'm sorry. If I can help you I'd be glad to. What cities in Europe?" Soon she and the singer were off in a deep discussion of places and schools and European singers and songs. The other girl was happy to just listen.

The first step and hurdle had been taken. Katherine's own good common sense and her new instinct for what might turn out to be a newspaper story told her that the best way to get to know the other students was to talk to them about themselves.

In the classrooms, in the cafeteria, in the gym, it was as if she had suddenly developed new ears and eyes. She learned to put names to faces so that she could remember them later. She found, to her great surprise, that many of the students knew of her from her story in the *Bridge*.

"Yet it's hard to make friends with them," she told Aunt Debra. "I'm looking for a good story for the *Bridge* and that means I'm talking to those who are active in clubs or leaders in the school or those who sing or dance or act in the Drama Club. They're all so busy. They all have friends. They're nice to me, but it isn't the same."

The telephone never rang for her at home. She could never fly down the stairs to pick up the receiver and hear Troy's voice —"Hi, Kit, what's doing? Finished your homework? Come on over"—or Flip calling to say, "Are you busy? I'm bored; I just want to talk for a few minutes" or Jet asking, "Do you really want to go to the movies Saturday night? I thought we could go ice-skating for a change."

She had told Aunt Debra about the break with the Crowd and confessed that she had gone on seeing Jet. Her aunt was sympathetic over the loss of Troy's friendship but she didn't spare Katherine's feelings when it came to Jet.

"That was a very bad thing you did, Katherine," she said sternly. "It was underhanded and sneaking. Perhaps I had no right to demand obedience from you, but I didn't know you as well then as I do now and I didn't know how to handle the situation. However"—she allowed herself to thaw—"you've admitted it; you've apologized. But what would your father have said about it?"

Katherine sat cross-legged on the sofa, in bathrobe and pajamas, pinning up her hair so she could brush out the curls smoothly in the morning. She sighed. "I was all mixed up. Daddy wrote me when I first came here, 'To thine own self be true'—and I thought that meant I should do just as I pleased. Now that I think of it, I wasn't being true to myself, let alone to you, when I went with Jet. I only went with him because the others took it for granted we would, and if I didn't I was afraid there'd be no place for me in their little, tight circle."

"Humph! Well, it's water under the bridge. Stop fussing with your hair. It's not bedtime yet. I'll teach you to play cribbage—if I can remember how, myself. It's been a long time."

She was offering the game as a sign of forgiveness. She was trying to be a companion and Katherine appreciated it. But playing cribbage with Aunt Debra was not the same as being with someone her own age.

The next day Flip spoke to her. It was the first time any of them had spoken to her that week. Flip had come up behind Katherine, who was examining the bulletin board, and remarked, "I just want to tell you how mean I think you are. Jet wasn't doing any harm; he was just having a little fun. Now he's going around like a thundercloud and everybody's miserable—just on account of you." She was gone before Katherine could say a word to her.

Katherine walked straight upstairs to the fourth floor and to the *Bridge* office. Bob happened to be alone when she went in and said, "I might as well tell you I've let you down, too. I can't find a story. I can't think of a thing. You're counting on me for the next issue and I've let you down."

"What are you talking about?" He stared at her, then got up from his desk and shook her gently by the shoulders. "I told you I'd help you with the first ones. Sure, I expect you to get your own stories later on; but as far as I'm concerned, you're a member of the staff now and we all help each other. Teamwork does it, up here. I thought you weren't interested or you were too busy—too many dates."

"I'm not seeing any of the Crowd. We aren't friends any more," she told him.

He whistled. "So that's why! I asked Troy last night why it was I hadn't seen you at the Macdonald house, running up the stairs with Troy, and she nearly bit my head off telling me it was none of my business. Never mind about that." He led her over to a desk. "This is an old, beat-up desk, but any time you want to use it, it's yours."

Hers. She was a member of the staff.

The reporter Audrey came in and Bob introduced them. "Katherine wrote that story 'Pies and a Pioneer,'" he explained.

"You're the mysterious author?" Audrey asked. "When Bob couldn't produce you, I claimed he'd stolen that story out of a book. Humble apologies, Bob."

"Just put your humble mind to helping us. We're trying to think up a new feature story for Katherine to write. How about a story on that kid—what's-his-name?—the freshman who's a mathematical wizard? He can just look at a column of figures, add it up in a second and give you the right answer."

Audrey shook her head. "I talked to him and there's no feature story there. The kid resents all the publicity he's getting; he hates it and wants to be treated like everybody else. Now I just saw the president of the Madrigal Society and—"

"She wants to know what we're going to say about the Madrigal this week. I've run a story on that and the A Capella every single issue. No. Absolutely no. If they'd give me something new and different about music and musicians, I'd print it." Bob sat down, leaned an elbow on his desk and propped his chin in his hand. "Think, kids. Think."

"There's a girl in my gym class," Katherine finally said, "who knows a lot about music, but not the madrigal kind. I started talking to her the other day and I found out that her father has one of the top jazz bands in San Francisco and she really knows all about it. She was trying to tell me the difference between progressive jazz and Dixieland and New Orleans and she really gave me an education. She's met most of the great jazz musicians and her father has a record collection that is priceless, she says."

"You see?" said Bob to Audrey, shaking his finger at her. "That's the difference between a genius and a muttonhead reporter like you. Katherine just happens to talk to somebody and picks up a terrific story."

The reporter threw an eraser at him. "Give me a good editor and I'd be a good reporter," she said, laughing, to Katherine. "Don't mind us. It is a good angle. 'Jazz Authority at Golden Gate Hi!' No, that's no good. Let Bob think up the title. That's his job."

"But I don't know anything about jazz. I could hardly understand what she was saying," Katherine protested.

"So much the better. The less you know, the better questions you'll ask. Tell her to give you the story as if she were spelling out the ABC's of it; then we'll know all the readers will understand it, not just the ones who already like progressive jazz." Bob had stopped kidding around and was speaking seriously. "Does this girl play any instrument herself? The saxophone? Better and better. I'm not going to tell you what kind of questions to ask or what kind of story to write. That would only cramp your style. Just do it your own way."

They were both looking at Katherine, expectantly, and she got up from the desk—her desk—where she had been lounging. "I know where that girl lives. She told me. If I go out there now, I may even catch her father at home and get to talk to him, since he works at night."

"Hah. A go-getter," said Audrey, but there was admiration as well as teasing in her tone.

Katherine came home at five-thirty with her head spinning jazz talk—the cool brilliance of progressive jazz; the counter-point of Dixieland, where each musician went off on his own yet each played the same tune. She had five pages filled with notes and she had her story.

And Aunt Debra had a job!

"It's only temporary, from now through the Christmas holi-days," she explained as they got dinner together. "Landero's Department Store always takes on extra help at this time. I'm not a private secretary; just a stenographer in the same room with ten other stenographers and we get called in whenever one of the executives wants to dictate. Quite a comedown for me, but I can't pick and choose. It's the only job I've been offered." She added, "Just before you came home Mr. Dale called. He's helping the new owners of the Marlborough and the new sec-retary couldn't locate the file on the orders we placed for twenty-five new mattresses. I tell you, I just itched to go over there and straighten things out! Why, that file was just where it should be. She must not be much good if she couldn't find it."

"Don't you give her a thought, or the Marlborough either. Let them find their own files!" Katherine was firm, because she knew how much and how wistfully Aunt Debra still thought about her old position.

"Listen to who is giving orders in this house!" Aunt Debra snorted. "There—I've made the cole slaw. Taste it. I suppose it won't be fancy enough for you."

Katherine tasted and shook her head. "What it needs is just a little bit of wine vinegar and—" She thought, and then said triumphantly, "A teaspoon of celery seed."

"You'll poison us both yet, with your ideas." Aunt Debra sprinkled the celery seed in, with the vinegar, and stirred the slaw vigorously. "Tell me more about this jazz story of yours. I never knew there were different kinds. To me it all sounds like a bunch of cats yelling on a back fence."

Katherine explained it again and found she was putting her own notes in order, almost writing her story in her head as she talked. "Can't I try to do it on the typewriter, Aunt Debra?" she asked when she finished. "I hate to give it to Bob in long-hand."

"I should say not. You're not ready yet. If you try to really type now, you'll start hunting and pecking instead of doing it right. You need lots and lots more practice."

She handed in her story to Bob and now she found that ideas were popping in her head. "With Christmas coming, how would it be if I took a sample poll through the school and found out what ten or twenty students wanted most for Christmas? Or if I asked them how they first found out there wasn't a Santa Claus?"

"I like the last idea best," Bob said. "The other's been done before. Oh, and, Katherine, could you come up on Thursday and help us? That's the day we go to press and we all pitch in. We have to correct the proofs from the printer to be sure it's absolutely perfect before it goes back to him for final printing. And there are always all kinds of emergencies—last-minute notices to jam in and things like that."

It was a madhouse, Thursday afternoon, but it was also the most fun she had ever had. How Jet and Flip would have hooted at the idea of work being fun! But it was. Audrey, Bob, the boy with the untidy hair, whose name turned out to be Jack Stuart, and a Negro boy, Richie Berlin, who was sports editor and also the high-school track star, and Katherine, herself, all pitched in and did everything that Bob told them to—but with a camaraderie and a teamwork and a lot of jokes that made the hour and a half just whizz by.

"Stop breathing down the back of my neck, Bob. I'll get this done," Audrey complained. "I can't read proof with you standing over me, giving me the jitters."

"You can't read, anyway," Richie told her. "You passed right over a line of type set upside down and didn't notice it. Upside-down Audrey. That's our girl."

"Huh. If you didn't grab so much space in the paper for your sports stories— Who reads them, anyway? It's my by-line everyone looks for. They say, 'That Audrey—now, there's a *reporter.*'"

"Ex-reporter, if she doesn't get to work." Bob winked at Katherine and brought over a page proof from the printer and his own pasted-up original from which the page had been made. "You read off every word, every comma, every single punctuation mark from my original and I check to see if the printer has put it all in, in this proof page."

They did that for a while. Then he switched sheets with her and showed her how to make the corrections in the margin. It was fascinating, like learning a code, because one squiggle meant that a letter had been left out of a word, and a different kind of squiggle meant that the word had been spelled wrong and then you had to spell it right in the margin. A straight line had to be placed if two words were jammed together without any space between them; a loop, with the pencil, over two letters meant those two letters had been reversed by the printer.

When it was all over and the paper was put to "bed"—sent back to the printer's again—they all trooped over to the Food Shop. Katherine was to learn this was a ritual on Thursday afternoons, but right now it seemed strange to be occupying the same big booth—but with a different group.

They all liked one another, this staff of the *Bridge.* They were friends. Sometimes their talk was just as silly as anything Binky or Flip ever said, but most of the time it was newspaper talk. In spite of their kidding they were all crazy about their work. Katherine listened and found she couldn't get enough of it; it was a tremendous thrill when they all raised their glasses of milk shake and toasted, "One more week—one more *Bridge* crossed!"

"Of course you liked it. That's what's called 'shop talk.'" Aunt Debra was exhausted that night and there was no typewriting lesson. She sat in the big chair with her feet up on the ottoman, but Katherine was delighted to see color in her face and her eyes alive. She had dreaded coming home to find her aunt despondent after her first day on the new job.

"Shop talk," Aunt Debra repeated. "Put two doctors in a roomful of people and they'll find each other and talk medicine. It's the same with any kind of work. You'd think secretaries like myself would get sick and tired of their jobs, but you just get a couple of us together and what do we talk about? Our jobs, our bosses, how we keep appointments straight and how we file and all the rest of it. So it's the same with your newspaper friends."

"How was your first day at Landero's?"

Aunt Debra rubbed the muscles at the back of her neck. "It's new and strange and that makes it difficult. But I can type as fast as the rest of them—faster, when it comes to columns of figures."

The telephone rang. Katherine answered it and came back into the room with such a radiance about her that her aunt noticed it. "Well, have you been made Queen of the May or something? I never saw such a silly look on anyone's face."

"I have a date for tomorrow," Katherine answered primly, "with Bob Macdonald. We're going out on a boat somewhere." She was so happy she couldn't contain it and she danced out of the room, pausing by her aunt's chair to give her cheek a swipe of a kiss before she ran upstairs.

Behind her she could hear the hoarse chuckle which was Aunt Debra's peculiar laughter.

10

The next day after school Bob was waiting for her and steered her over to a car. "I borrowed it and I hope it runs. We're going to the Yacht Basin."

"That sounds so grand," she said.

"Are you thinking of big, million-dollar yachts?" They were driving up one hill and down the next, headed for the bay. "It's not all that grand. Mostly they are small boats—sailboats and motorboats—and people use them to go out in the bay on week ends. They can go over to Sausalito or Belvedere or just drift around. I'm sorry it's such a foggy day." Bob peered anxiously ahead at the thick gray fog which hung low over the water.

They parked the car and walked a block to a broad avenue, heavy with traffic, and on the other side of it the water; not blue today but steel-gray. As soon as the traffic lights changed, Bob grabbed her hand and they ran across together. From somewhere they could hear the deep, solemn tones of the foghorns. Katherine shivered.

"When I first came here I hated those foghorns. I'd hear them at night and they'd make me feel so lonesome and afraid."

"Honest?" He was astonished. "You never gave me the impression you were afraid of anything. I like the foghorns. I've grown up with them. Here we are. Hey! Can we come aboard?" He led her down the wharf to the small green sailboat with a cabin in its center. "I know my friend's here because his dog's here. Down, Mr. Bailey, down!" He patted the mastiff's rough coat and the dog licked his hand.

A man stuck his head out of the cabin. It was Mr. Bean.

Both he and Bob were pleased at Katherine's surprise. "I

told Bob not to let you know it was my boat; I wanted to keep it a secret. I thought to myself, She's such a nice girl and always so pretty and dainty, she'll wonder what kind of boat a postman would have. Some old tub, dirty and full of splinters." He glanced around while Katherine protested, and it was obvious he was bursting with pride at the sleekness, the cleanness and trimness of his green boat.

"I think it's wonderful, Mr. Bean. And thank you so much for inviting me."

"You being a furriner and all, I don't suppose you've ever done any sailing?" Mr. Bean asked her.

Katherine smiled. Did he think there were no boats and no water in all of Europe—no Mediterranean? But she only said, "Very little, I'm afraid. I don't know much about boats."

"It doesn't look as if we'll get any sailing today unless this fog lifts." Bob was disappointed.

"Come down in the cabin and have a sandwich, anyways," Mr. Bean invited them. "No, I don't mean you, Mr. Bailey. There's not room below for us and a dog, too. Not this time. No, I don't think we'll sail. That fog's thickening and there's no wind. We'd get out there and get becalmed and just drift around all night. Too dangerous." He led the way down the narrow steps and into the small galley.

It was all neat and shipshape. A small stove; a few shelves where plastic dishes were ranged, carefully protected by thin railings of wood so they wouldn't slip out. Through an open door Katherine could glimpse two bunks, one above the other. There was even a small curved bench where she could sit, squeezed against some old clothes of Mr. Bean that hung from the wall.

They ate ham sandwiches and drank hot chocolate which Mr. Bean made for them. It was so cozy and so unusual a place that Katherine was enchanted with it and didn't mind a bit that they couldn't sail out into the bay. The fog seemed to shut them into a world of their own; the boat rocked a little in its anchorage; she could look out of the porthole and see a great, ghostly shape of a freighter just going by. Mr. Bean took the scraps of the ham out to feed his dog and she and Bob were alone.

It was the nicest and oddest date she had ever had.

They washed the cups at the sink and carefully put them away in their places on the shelf. They talked. They stood at the porthole together, close together, not speaking but just watching the thick, slowly drifting fog, and she liked Bob's arm around her shoulder.

"Would you rather go some place else?" he asked once. "This isn't very exciting for you."

"I'd rather be here than any place else. Look, Bob, Mr. Bean even has a two-shelf refrigerator. It's like a toy."

"Did you see the little bunk he has in there for the dog? Mr. Bean lives with his sister, but I think he sleeps here and cooks for himself here on this boat a lot of the time. He loves it. Even on days like this he comes down and tinkers around. He's up above, now, going over every inch of the boat to see if it needs new paint, just as happy as he can be." Mr. Bailey was barking furiously and Bob smiled. "That dog has a perpetual feud with sea gulls. He knows he can't catch them, but just the same he tries every time he sees one. They aren't going to light on *his* boat, not if *he* has anything to say about it."

As Aunt Debra could have predicted, she and Bob talked "shop." They went up on the deck and Bob wrapped Mr. Bean's old duffel coat around her so that she would be warm and he pretended—to Mr. Bean—that he was helping examine the deck for paint scratches, as they stretched out on the flat surface. Actually Bob could see only about four feet of deck space ahead of him and his hand moved idly over the scratches. He was thinking about newspapers.

"I don't remember when I didn't want to work on a paper," he told her. "It was my ambition ever since I was a kid. Troy was going to draw the cartoons and I was going to be the reporter. What about you? Do you want to be a reporter?"

"There are just two things I like to do—write stories and cook. And I don't know which I like best," she said.

They were lying with their elbows propped up on pillows. Now he moved slightly so that he could look at her; his face was only inches away from hers. "You're lucky. You have a special talent if you want a career and another talent if you'd rather get married."

It had an echo, it seemed to her. Get married—get married—get married. She couldn't speak because her throat was suddenly tight. Of course she had thought of marriage before. There was a rosy, nebulous dream of herself in a white wedding gown; but it had never been real, nor had there been a picture of the man at her side. Now it did seem real and possible and something that could happen to her, just because Bob had said those words, just because he was so close to her and he was real.

Don't be an idiot, she thought. He isn't proposing. He has to go to college and so do you.

Fortunately Mr. Bean called to Bob, "Come here, Bob, and look at this. Remember two weeks ago when we bumped the wharf? There's a bad scratch, right down to the wood, below the water line."

Bob crawled over to see and Katherine sat up, then stood up. She balanced herself, carefully, against the rocking of the boat and the slightly sloping deck. This was no big yacht, as Bob had said; this was a small boat and there was no railing at the edge, just a thin rope which ran all around the outside edge about a foot from the deck.

"Watch Mr. Bailey!" she called, laughing. "He's trying to catch that sea gull."

Mr. Bean shook his head. "Fool dog. Wouldn't you think he'd learn some sense by now?" Then both he and Bob went back to examine the scratch, their legs on the deck and their heads far over the side, peering down.

From where Katherine stood she could almost see the hills of San Francisco. At moments the fog would lift and then it was like a curtain going up on a stage play: she could see homes and buildings and lights in the windows and the heights of the hills. The fog would close down again and there was no San Francisco, just herself standing on a rocking boat in the middle of nowhere.

"Be quiet, Mr. Bailey," she shushed him. His barking distracted her from the unearthly beauty around her. She took another small step nearer the side.

The sea gull chose that moment to dive in toward the boat. Behind her she could hear Mr. Bailey's frantic, wild yapping, but she was interested only in the bird because he had soared to a position right in front of her face and was holding himself stationary there, flapping his wings. She could see his beak and his eyes and his white wings; she could almost reach out and touch him.

The dog, racing toward the gull, hit her legs with all his force. Off balance, she felt herself lurch forward and clutched wildly in the air for support—but there was no support. Her knees hit the board deck and she slid; the small rope barrier was no barrier at all, but rather a catapult that threw her headlong over the side.

Katherine hit the water with a resounding splash. It was icy-cold and paralyzing. She went down, deep down, weighted with her clothes and the extra heaviness of the duffel jacket. Water choked her mouth and nose. Shock almost caused her to faint.

Then, instinctively, she flailed around with her arms and legs and came to the surface with a strangling cry. She couldn't see but she could hear a voice yelling 'Katherine!' and another one crying, 'Hold on! Hold on! We'll get you!' "

Hold on to what? was the only rational thought she had before the water engulfed her again and she was sinking with the drag of her soaked clothes and struggling to rise by kicking her arms and thrashing her legs. She couldn't swim—not in this bitterly cold water and in so many clothes. She could only flounder.

When two strong arms went around her waist she tried to fight against them, too, before she realized that this was Bob and this was rescue. He pulled her to the surface and got her head above water. He treaded water for a second, asking anxiously, "Are you all right?" She nodded her head, sputtering out water from her mouth. Then he swam the few feet to the boat and pushed her ahead of him so that Mr. Bean could reach down and pull her up onto the boat.

The first thing she saw was Mr. Bailey. He was cowering and he was as dripping wet as she was; evidently he, too, had fallen in.

"That dog," Mr. Bean said, patting her on the back while she coughed up salty water. "That stupid dog! I heard you scream and looked up and all I saw was your feet going over the side and Mr. Bailey right behind you. I know he must have knocked you over—he was so excited about that bird."

"Did—did—I scream?" Katherine was shivering so violently and her throat was so raw she could hardly get the words out. "I'm all—all—right. Now." She started to laugh, almost hysterically. "I'm a mess. L-look at me. I'm so wet—" Bob was rubbing her hands, hard.

Quickly Mr. Bean took charge. "Both of you get down to the cabin. You're both soaked and in this cold air you could catch pneumonia. I'm glad you can laugh, Katherine. Can't be too much wrong with you if you can laugh."

He shut the door in between the galley and the sleeping bunks. Bob could get into some of Mr. Bean's things, but the older man ordered her, through the closed door, to take off her wet clothes and climb into a bunk. In a few seconds she had done as he ordered, rubbing herself to a warm glow with rough towels, then crawled inside the blankets. The door opened just wide enough for Mr. Bean to throw in a clean shirt of his which she pulled over her head.

Bob knocked. "How are you doing?"

"Fine. Come in." She was sitting up in bed, toweling her hair, which was a mass of curling red, wet ringlets. "This is so warm—I know now what they mean by 'snug as a bug in a rug.' That's just how I feel. Glorious! Oh, Bob, that water was cold."

"I know. I was in it." He made a face. "This is some fine date for you, a ducking in San Francisco Bay." He sat down, hard, on the edge of the bunk and let out his breath as if he'd been holding it in ever since he heard Katherine scream. "Wow! I was scared stiff. I ran over to the side of the boat but I couldn't see you for a moment—I guess you were down at the bottom and the water's that funny gray color so it was hard to see anything. Then, when you did come up, you were over to my left and I didn't expect to see you there. By the time I jumped in you'd gone down again."

"But you did jump in. Thanks, Bob. You'll never know how wonderful it felt to know you had me and I was saved."

"Ordinarily it isn't dangerous here, not in the summertime. The water's always cold but you can swim in it."

"Lean over," she commanded. "Your hair is still wet and it's dripping down the back of your neck." She used another towel, rubbing so hard his hair stuck up in spikes. "Look at you! Your hair's all on end and your arms are at least four inches longer than Mr. Bean's and they stick out of his shirt sleeves. Speaking of that, look at me in his shirt. What am I going to do? My clothes won't ever get dry and I can't put those wet things back on again."

"You're right. Beanie!" he called.

"Yes? I'm making more hot chocolate," he called from the galley.

Bob stood in the doorway between the two tiny rooms and talked to them both. "I'm going to take the car and run home and see what I can find of Troy's clothes that would fit Katherine. I'll ask Mom to help me—she knows about such things. All right, Katherine?"

"That would be fine."

"Then get going." Mr. Bean had the chocolate on a tray but he couldn't pass Bob; the space was too small. "Let **Dr.** Bean get in there to take care of his patient." He squeezed in as Bob got out, and set the tray carefully on the bunk.

After Bob left, the two of them sat and sipped the hot sweet liquid in companionable silence. Then Mr. Bean chuckled. "You sure looked funny when we dragged you out of the water. Like a wet sack of laundry. Are you sure you aren't hurt any place? You didn't bump yourself?"

"Nothing's hurt but my pride, Mr. Bean. Today of all days— when I wanted to look my best." There was such a kindly humor in Mr. Bean that it loosened his tongue.

"You like Bob, don't you? That's all right—because I think he likes you, too. He's a good boy. He always got into his share of trouble, but not through meanness—not that one. I take an interest in all the young people on my mail route and I've watched Bob and Theresa grow up. They used to be so close. Stick together, those two? Why, glue wasn't in it with them. Not any more; I guess when kids grow up to be your age they've got to strike out on their own and they want to be different."

"Yes," she argued, "but Troy—Theresa—wants to be different and yet she's afraid to be different." Katherine was actually thinking out loud. "She and her whole Crowd talk and talk about not wanting to be sheep, like the rest of the students, but that's just what they are. They go round and round doing the same old things, while Bob is different without thinking about it or talking about it; he's *himself.*"

"It's a problem, Katherine. At your age it's natural that you should be feeling your oats. You're almost grown up—but not quite." He lit his pipe, stretched out his legs and propped his back against the foot of the bunk. "Trouble is, some kids figure it out all wrong. They want to start thinking for themselves so they say the heck with the teachers and the parents; but then they turn right around and substitute what their **gang** thinks, as the authority over them. Hey—here's someone come in to see you. Mr. Bailey, you come right in and apologize to the lady."

The dog slunk in, his big, brown eyes searching Katherine's wistfully. She extended her hand. "Come on, Mr. Bailey. I'm not angry with you; but the next time you pick a fight with a sea gull, I'm going to be nowhere, just nowhere, around."

"You're talking real good American, aren't you? You've lost that funny little accent you had and you're picking up the slang," Mr. Bean commented.

"I try. But it's hard. I listen and listen but sometimes I say it all wrong. Troy called me one night and said, 'Let's yak awhile.' I didn't know what she meant. So I asked her what was a yak and she laughed. And Chap was kidding Jet one night and Jet said, 'Oh, get off my back'—but Chap wasn't even touching him."

There were sounds of footsteps overhead, then coming down the steps. "Here comes Bob, now. I hope he brought something that fits," she said.

Bob was coming down the stairs and Troy was with him, carrying a small, packed suitcase in her hand.

"Wait a minute," Mr. Bean called out. "Four of us won't fit in here. Hello, Troy. I think us men had better get out of here."

So it was Troy who came in all alone and closed the door behind her. "All right, Kit? I've brought stockings, shoes, dress —everything. Bob had us so scared. He charged into the house and we couldn't make any sense out of what he was saying; something about an accident—that you had drowned—that you had fallen overboard—that he was afraid you'd get sick and die. I was scared."

Katherine laughed. "Look at me. Safe and sound."

"Good. Well, let's see how these things fit. I'm taller than you are, so everything may be a bit too large." Troy had never resembled her brother as much as she did then, ordering Katherine around, taking charge, tying a loop in a shoulder strap and, finally, sitting Katherine down on the bunk and

149

combing her hair. "It's almost dry but I can't fix the bangs. They're frizzy now, so I'll just have to pull them straight back." This was the way Bob acted in the editorial office: giving orders but good-naturedly doing most of the work himself.

"You should see my bedroom," she said. "Bob went dashing up the stairs with me behind him and before I could stop him he had thrown most of my clothes from the closet onto the bed. I had to calm that boy down before I could find out what he was doing. There, you're all finished."

All dressed, Katherine stood up and faced Troy. Suddenly all the painful memories, the hurt and the anger between them, came back.

"Troy, I do wish we were still friends."

"So do I," Troy answered, but her features hardened. "It's your choice. You were the one to break it up, and I mean you *have* broken things up. Jet just hasn't been the same. I think he's determined to show you or prove something to you, but anyway he's going to run for vice-president of the senior class. It's just ridiculous. He has as much business being a class officer as Mr. Bailey. It's changed things for all of us; nothing is any fun any more. Just the same, we're all behind him. He's our Jet and if he wants to be vice-president, we'll see to it he is vice-president."

"You can't blame me for what Jet is doing," Katherine protested.

"I do blame you. Kit, you were the best friend I ever had. I liked you much more than I did Flip or Binky or any of the others. How could you accuse Jet of outright stealing? *Stealing.*"

She says it too violently, too emphatically, Katherine thought. She's trying to convince herself; she isn't sure about Jet either, but that silly business of being loyal just because you're one of the Crowd makes her determined to think I'm wrong.

"Maybe he wasn't," Katherine said, "but he went so close to it—anyway, Troy, it isn't Jet. I'd like to have you for my best friend, but I don't want to be part of a little clique that keeps me apart from the rest of the school."

"Then," said Troy bitterly, with her back to Katherine as she fumbled to open the door, "then Flip was right. You never really did belong with us."

It was a silent ride home. Bob tried to make conversation as they left the boat but he soon saw that both girls were too upset to talk. He asked no questions. He didn't want to take sides.

He stopped the car in front of the Macdonald house. Troy got out as quickly as she could.

"Thanks for lending me these clothes, Troy. I'll return—"

"You're welcome," Troy said, and ran up her steps.

Bob walked across the street with Katherine and they had to stop twice to rescue a shoe that came off, since Troy's were too large for Katherine's feet. The incidents made them laugh and some of the heavy load around Katherine's heart lightened a little.

"I don't imagine you feel much like going out tonight, but how about the movies tomorrow night?" Bob asked. "I promise no water and no sea gulls and no Mr. Bailey."

He held her hand in the movies that night and she liked it. The touch of Bob's thin, strong fingers around hers was both nice and disturbing—so much so that sometimes she lost track of what was happening on the screen. Once in a while his fingers moved to stroke hers or pinch them lightly.

He didn't try to kiss her when he took her home. That was disappointing. He had made a move to do it, then checked himself. "Good night, Katherine," he said, in a very special voice. "Do I have a date for next Friday night? And the Friday after that? Would you give a little thought to going steady with me?"

Her forehead puckered up. "I'm not sure I know what it means to go steady. Jet used to say I was going steady with him, but I never had any dates, alone, with him."

"Did he ever kiss you—or shouldn't I ask?"

151

"I wouldn't let him." Her voice was full of indignation.

Bob laughed. "You weren't going steady. If we do, then you're my girl and nobody else's. I couldn't ask you before because, until you started working at the *Bridge,* you wouldn't have understood how many hours I have to spend there and maybe you'd have been sore about it. This way we'll spend as much free time as we have together, but we'll understand if the other one has to work or study. You'll think about it?"

"Men are silly." She tossed back her head. "I don't have to think about it. Of course I'll go steady with you."

He reached for her, then, but she laughed, gave him a push and slammed the door in his face. Behind it she could hear him call, "Okay—you wait."

It was December now and, on that Monday, Katherine could feel the tempo of school quickening. Exams were approaching; talk of school elections was in the air; the excitement of Christmas was not far off.

In her registry room—in that usual ten minutes before classes —the teacher took the attendance check, made an announcement that the meeting of the Future Teachers Association was shifted from Mondays to Wednesdays, then she reported: "Class elections will be held in two weeks. The names of the candidates will be posted on the bulletin board; you will have the opportunity of hearing them speak at assemblies, but I will read them off now:

"For President: Manuel Perada and James Hill. For Vice-President: Marguerite Kelley and John Smith—"

She looked up. "It says, in parentheses here, 'Jet' Smith."

After that, Katherine scarcely listened to the others. So Jet was going to run. She resented it fiercely. She wanted to stand up in front of the class and say, 'He doesn't mean it. He isn't serious about it. It's a joke with him or a dare or he's trying to show off." But she couldn't do that.

"What do you think are his chances?" she asked Marguerite

that afternoon while they were both trying to get a drink of water at the fountain. "Jet can't possibly win, can he? He's never done anything in school affairs before. He's always sneered at them."

"Don't fool yourself. A lot of the kids think he's handsome and glamorous and that he's kind of a rebel. It appeals to them." Marguerite got water on her chin and wiped it off with her handkerchief. "He has his own friends who'll do nothing for the next weeks but work for him and tell everybody how wonderful he is. My trouble, Bob says, is that I don't loosen up and laugh more. He wants me to make jokes but I don't know how. I guess I haven't much of a sense of humor."

So in addition to trying to make new friends for herself, trying to get stories from them for the *Bridge,* Katherine had a new motive for boldly speaking to strangers. She was electioneering for Marguerite. In her English Lit class the ice had been broken a little between herself and Troy; no longer did Troy sit with rigid head, looking straight ahead. The two girls exchanged hellos, if nothing else. What bothered Katherine was how good a job Troy was doing for Jet.

"He has ideas!" Troy said to the girl on their left, and Katherine couldn't help overhearing. "If Jet's elected, our graduation and our graduation dance will be sensational. He has new ideas. Marguerite will give us the same old stuff."

Katherine saw a cartoon Troy had drawn which passed all around the room—a caricature of Marguerite, emphasizing all of her worst points: her solemn expression, her deep-set eyes, her humorless mouth. It showed none of Marguerite's kindness and goodness and competence.

There was nothing wrong with Troy's campaigning. She had as much right to campaign for Jet as Katherine had for Marguerite. Katherine was just afraid Troy and Flip and the others were doing too good a job of it.

"I know what you mean," said Mary Michaelson, the star in the play the Drama Club was planning. Katherine had just finished interviewing her for her feature article "How Did You Learn about Santa Claus?" and they had begun to talk about the class elections. "Usually no one pays a lot of attention to the race between the vice-presidents. It's always the president who gets the attention. This time all you hear around school is Jet Smith and Marguerite Kelley."

"Whom are you going to vote for?" Katherine asked. "Marguerite has proved herself. She's always helping people. When I first came here to Golden Gate and I didn't know anyone, the first question she asked me was what could she do to help me."

"I know, but I haven't made up my mind yet. They're making such a fuss over this Jet, I figure he must have something." The young actress looked at her, strangely. "Didn't you used to go around with Jet? I've seen you with him."

"Yes, and believe me he won't stick with the job if he's elected. I know him. He'll soon get bored and that will be the end of it." Katherine got to her feet. The two girls had been sitting out on the lawn by the side of the school. "I have to get busy and interview more people."

"Who else? I thought that was such a silly question when you asked me when I first learned there was no Santa Claus, but I can see you could make a cute story out of it. When we moved to that apartment when I was six years old, and I saw there was no fireplace chimney and yet there were presents the next morning, then I knew."

Katherine said, "I'd like to ask Sandra Colbin. She's a junior and the real school beauty, but I don't know her."

"I do," Mary said. "I'll take you over now and introduce you."

So one by one Katherine was getting to know many of the students, especially the active ones, the ones who were leaders or had some special ability or talent. She interviewed Dean Dower, the football quarterback; the editor of the school yearbook; the president of the Tri-Y; a freshman girl who had won a prize in a nationwide cake-baking contest; a sister and a brother who sang comic songs together at assemblies; two of the teachers.

When her story was finished she took it up to the *Bridge* office.

It was Wednesday and Bob was sitting at his desk writing furiously. He glanced up as she came in. He threw down his pencil and jumped to his feet.

"Katherine! Did Jack find you? I sent him looking for you."

She shook her head and put her story in the basket on his desk. "No, why?"

"Because I'm in trouble and you're the only one that can help me. Audrey was supposed to do an interview with both Marguerite and Jet, on what their program would be. Jack Stuart is getting the information from the candidates for president and secretary and treasurer; but Audrey's job was the vice-presidents, because that's the race everyone's talking about. And Audrey's sick. Her mother just telephoned that she couldn't come to school today—this is the first I heard of it."

"Can't Richie—"

"Richie always works after school on Wednesdays; he has a job in a filling station."

Katherine looked at her editor with dismay. "Bob, I can't interview Jet. You don't know what you're asking. Marguerite, yes. I'll go see her, but I don't want to talk to Jet. I never told you, but we had a quarrel."

"I guessed that." He walked up and down the office, his hands jammed in his pockets. He started to speak and then stopped. Katherine guessed he was hunting for some way to persuade her and she stiffened in protest. She wouldn't do it!

Bob slammed his hand down on a pile of old newspapers. "You have to. There's no one else. You're a member of the staff here and personal feelings just don't count. These interviews will be the whole front page. I've saved space for Marguerite and Jet. I can't write it; I would if I could. But I have to be here and spend every minute rewriting and editing the stories as they come in, seeing that they fit into the space on the front page—not to mention all I have to do on the other pages."

"Can't Richie or Jack do it tomorrow? Maybe Audrey won't be sick then."

He shook his head. "Can't take the chance. Jack's too busy. That's out. Audrey may still be sick tomorrow. I can't reach Richie now, so I don't know what his plans are for tomorrow; not all the sports stories are in and I've a hunch he's working on a basketball spread. You are the only one of the staff who is free, Katherine."

It was such fun being on the staff; but it couldn't be all fun, she realized. It carried a responsibility, too.

She made one last protest. "Jet hates me. Of that whole Crowd, Troy's the only one who will even speak to me. Suppose he refuses the interview?"

"He won't. He wants to win that office. Besides"—Bob was smiling now and the smile deepened the little crease in his cheek; his eyes were grateful—"a good newspaperwoman always gets her story. Go out there and fight, team."

As she turned to go, he called after her, "There's a deadline. I have to get it to the printer's early tomorrow afternoon, at the very latest."

11

It was three-thirty now and the school was almost deserted. By luck she ran into Marguerite just outside Mr. Johns's office and got her story. There was nothing very original in Marguerite's platform but it was sincere: good student government, encouragement of more students into club activity; special attention to Brotherhood Week in February. Marguerite's pet project was a special dance by the senior class to raise money to buy a tape recorder so that all their graduation exercises, all their voices and special messages to each other at graduation could be recorded. Then each member would have a tape record to keep.

"People hang on to their yearbooks all their lives. Why shouldn't we hear our own voices and those of our friends? Senior graduation is so important," Marguerite said.

"I'll put that in the story as a direct quote from you," Katherine promised.

Jet was nowhere around. She asked a few students and one remembered seeing him go off in his car.

As soon as she reached home she telephoned him. There was no answer and she knew that the weak feeling she had was relief because the interview could be postponed. She dreaded talking to him. She called across the street but Troy wasn't there either. There was no telling where the Crowd was. Well, she'd put it off until tomorrow morning.

Aunt Debra came in. Katherine noticed there was a spring to her step and that she bustled around, energetically, as she took off her hat and coat, smoothed down her hair and started for the kitchen.

"Did you peel the potatoes?" she asked.

"Not yet, Aunt Debra. How's the job? You look as if something nice has happened."

"Nothing special. Oh, you ironed the aprons! Good. Tie mine, will you? I'm getting into the swing of things at Landero's and I must say I didn't know a department store could be so interesting. Downstairs, everything's Christmas, Christmas, Christmas—all the decorations up and the crowds swarming in, but upstairs we are already thinking ahead to January sales. Today I took dictation from the head of the advertising department. He called me *four* times—asked specially for me. The reason he did, I think, is because I made a suggestion he liked, the first time. It wasn't anything remarkable; just the sort of thing I used to do at the Marlborough. He was dictating a memo to the general manager and I asked him if he didn't want copies made for the Art Department and the Sales Department, since it concerned all three. He said yes and thanked me for the idea."

"Is the work hard?" Katherine asked.

"Not hard enough," the older woman sniffed. "I like something I can get my teeth into, with responsibility. Oh, we work at a fast pace; there's plenty to do and I'm learning something new every day and there are always emergencies—shipments don't come in on time, or it's the wrong order, or we find we haven't stocked enough talking dolls and everybody wants talking dolls. Or our Santa Claus gets laryngitis, as he did yesterday."

Katherine looked at her aunt with affection and pride, over the bowl of potatoes she was peeling. Aunt Debra had landed squarely on her feet, and now she was talking about Landero's just the way she used to talk about the Marlborough. *"We,"* she was saying. *Our* Santa Claus.

"Speaking of Christmas," Katherine said, "where will we put our own Christmas tree? In the bay window or against the wall by the small chair?"

"Now, Katherine, don't start that. I'm not going to have any

Christmas tree in here, dropping pine needles all over the rug and making a lot of extra work. I'm much too busy at the store to be bothered and you have too much schoolwork. We'll hang some lights in the window and that's all." Aunt Debra opened the oven door to see if the roast was coming along all right, carefully closed it and took off her apron. "When you finish put the potatoes on to boil and then we can rest until dinner's ready. I'm going to lie down for half an hour."

Katherine slashed so angrily at the potato she was holding that she cut it almost in half, peel and all. No Christmas tree! And she had been looking forward to it with such excitement. Her father had promised her, "Wait until you see a real American Christmas with all the trimmings—tree and everything." Now there wouldn't be any tree.

Wasn't she unhappy enough? Wasn't it enough that she had to face Jet tomorrow? She knew and dreaded just how he would act: mocking and unpleasant. He would find some way to say something to embarrass her. She knew him. And very likely one of the Crowd would be hanging around with him and she'd have to face him, too.

She was silent and moody all during dinner. When Aunt Debra suggested, afterward, that they have a lesson on the typewriter, Katherine answered shortly, "I can't. I have too much homework." She marched upstairs and thought to herself, I don't care if I am acting badly. I don't care if I hurt her feelings. Why can't we have a Christmas tree like everyone else?

She tried not to think about tomorrow and Jet and concentrate on studying, but it was no use. Maybe Flip, with that quick, malicious tongue of hers, would be there, too. Or Troy, looking disdainful. If this was what it meant to be a newspaperwoman, she wasn't sure it was something she wanted to be.

Almost the first person she saw at school the next morning was Jet. She gathered her courage and made her way resolutely toward him.

"Jet, may I talk to you? I want to get a story—"

"Can't you see I'm busy? I'm talking to Chap." The two of them turned their backs and walked quickly away.

So it was going to be worse than she had thought. Jet was downright rude. She would have to force herself on him. His next class was physics and she waited for him outside the door. He came out surrounded by five students, all of them laughing at something he had said.

"Jet, I must see you. I want an interview for the *Bridge*. I've already talked to Marguerite, and if you won't give me a story we'll just print her election platform and not yours." It was a threat she was making and he stopped short.

"All right," he drawled. "But not now; there isn't time. You know where to find me at lunch time. We'll talk then."

Oh, no! She couldn't go to the Food Shop and talk to him surrounded by the whole Crowd.

Bob caught her just before eleven. "Do you have those stories?" He was worried. "The other pages have all gone to the printer and we'll have page proofs on them by this afternoon. But I've held up the front page."

"I have an appointment with Jet at noon." There was no getting out of it now.

"Good." He exhaled with relief. "I'll be waiting in the office. Rush it up to me before the lunch hour is over, will you? I'll get permission to cut my first afternoon class and I can get it over to the printer's."

When lunch time came she walked over to the Food Shop, down past the counter to the big table at the back. They were all there, every one of them.

"Look who's coming," said Candy.

"Look who the cat dragged in," said Flip.

"She's going to interview me," mocked Jet. "See the nice sharp pencils she has? And all that clean paper? I'm going to talk and she's going to take down every priceless word that drips from my tongue. Aren't you, Kit?"

160

"Quit clowning," Chap advised. "I'm your campaign manager and you've got to make a good impression in the *Bridge*."

"She doesn't want to know what you're going to do if you're elected; she wants to ask you when you first learned there wasn't any Santa Claus." George Yale's voice was spiteful and he was pretending to lisp in baby talk. "Did you know there wasn't any Santa Claus, Jet?"

"No! You kidding? Then who brings all the Easter bunnies?" Jet said, and it was good for a laugh from everybody but Chap and Troy. Troy had her head down and wouldn't look at Kit.

Katherine had been standing all this time. She was so humiliated that her face was burning; there were tears behind her eyelids; her hands were shaking.

"I have to get this story, Jet." There was a funny something in her throat and she could hardly speak. "Bob's waiting for it, to take to the printer's."

"Well, go ahead. Ask me questions." He sprawled on the seat bench. "Go ahead." Even if she had wanted to sit down, there was no room.

"Oh, don't even talk to her." That was Binky.

"Sure, why not?" Pedro laughed. "Jet has a terrific program: five weeks' holiday at Christmas, two months at Easter. No exams, ever. *Real* student government—we tell the teachers what to do."

"Why bother to talk to her?" Binky insisted. "She's on Marguerite Kelley's side. Whatever you give her, Jet, won't make any difference. She'll write the story so that Marguerite's a doll and you're a jerk."

That did it. Katherine forgot to be humiliated; she was so angry.

"If I write a story, it's an honest story," she snapped. "All Jet has to do is start talking and I'll take it down just as he says it. You can just forget my name is Katherine Norman. Right now I'm a reporter."

No one said a word, but Troy raised her head and gave Katherine a slow look of approval.

Finally Chap spoke up. "I'll give you the program. I'm the campaign manager. The first thing he's proposing is a get-together party right after the holidays. No one comes with a date and no one can dance with the same person more than twice. That will get the senior class feeling like they really belong to one another, and bring the shy ones out."

It was a good suggestion, Katherine felt as she scribbled notes fast. But it was a strange one, coming from this clique that stayed off by themselves.

Chap went on to talk of Jet's plans for the senior class graduation, the banquet, the program. When he had finished, Katherine turned to Jet. "I have a direct quote from Marguerite. It's only fair that I get one from you. You know, *Jet Smith said* ... quote."

"There are a lot of complaints about the photographer who took last year's class pictures. If I'm elected, I'll see to it we have a good photographer." Jet proclaimed it as arrogantly as if he were already elected.

Smart, she thought. There had been a lot of complaints. That would appeal to the seniors.

"All right. That's all there will be space for." She folded up her notes. "Thank you for being so polite."

"Miaow," George Yale yelled after her.

In the *Bridge* office Bob looked up and whistled. "You look as if you've been fighting a war. Your red hair's giving off sparks and so are your eyes."

"Well, I think I won a battle," but she didn't tell him any more than that. If it weren't for Troy she would have spilled it all to Bob, but she couldn't include his sister in her general indignation. While Bob edited and corrected the story she had already written on Marguerite, she wrote up the one on Jet. She and Bob shared a sandwich he had brought and they said very little, but the good feeling that flowed between them, as they worked, eased her heart.

It had hurt, standing there seeing all her old friends being so nasty—even Troy hadn't taken her part and it was Troy she really missed. She had no close girl friend, and she didn't want anyone except Troy.

Just the same, in spite of the humiliation and the anger, she felt as if she had won a victory. The old, terrible need to belong was gone; she was happier, much happier, working here with Bob than when she had been part of the noon gathering at the Food Shop. When the bell rang and it was time for class, her story was finished and she gave it to him.

"Good girl," he said. "Will you come up this afternoon to correct proof?"

"I wouldn't miss it," she answered.

"This issue"—he rattled the page—"begins the fireworks. Next week they'll all be campaigning. They'll all speak at assemblies and they'll be making posters and election placards. We'll see some action."

That Friday night Bob kissed her, but for some reason she was suddenly both shy and awkward. She turned her head away.

"What's the matter, Katherine?" he asked softly.

"Nothing. I don't know. I'm sorry."

He gave her shoulder a squeeze. "Don't be. Never pays to rush things. When you want to kiss me, I'll know it. Good night, Katherine."

The next week all the candidates were presented at a senior class assembly and they all made speeches. It worried Katherine that Marguerite Kelley looked so plain and undistinguished up on the platform and that she spoke so matter-of-factly. What she said was good, but did it impress anyone? When Jet got up right afterward, handsome, smiling, charming, making a special compliment to his opponent's fine record and apologizing that he had never, himself, gone in for politics before, she knew how insincere he was. She knew he meant no real compliment to Marguerite. But did the other students know it?

Jet had a magnetism that reached out and made everyone in the audience feel as if he were speaking just to that one person, alone. Even Katherine, knowing him so well, could feel it. He told a few jokes and really made them all laugh; he was just serious enough and modest enough and self-confident enough to make her think his chances of winning were very good.

For the next few days it seemed to Katherine that everywhere she looked, in the halls, there were Jet and Chap, or Flip and Troy, or Pedro or Toby or Binky, buttonholing students and talking to them—and there was no question what they were talking about: Jet's candidacy.

The Art Department set aside one room where all the supporters of all the candidates could work, making posters and signs. There was a lot of hilarious business, keeping each one's secret from the other. Posters were stacked against the wall, their painted sides hidden, and no one was supposed to look at them. They had to be passed on by teachers appointed for that purpose.

Katherine often walked by this room, since it was just opposite Miss Sunderman's classroom and she seldom failed to find Troy in there. Troy was a clever comic artist and she was using these talents now to make posters for Jet. The fat artist who drew cartoons for the *Bridge* was doing the same for Marguerite.

The staff of the *Bridge* had to be neutral—in the paper—but that didn't mean they couldn't work for their candidates as private individuals.

The next Friday the elections would be held, by secret ballot, in the registry ten-minute periods. The day before, the posters would go up, in specially designated places, all around the school and school yard. They could not go up earlier because the school faculty knew that the excitement would grow, once the posters were seen, and this would interfere with studying for examinations, which would follow the next week.

That Wednesday, Katherine's registry teacher told her, "Mr. Johns would like to see you this morning. You'll be excused from your first study period."

"Hello, Katherine," he greeted her when she walked into Room 112. It had familiar echoes of that first day except that Mr. Johns was more relaxed. He was swinging, slightly, from side to side in his swivel chair, leaning back with his hands locked behind his head. He smiled at her. "I've rather expected to see you here before; I thought there might be problems or questions I could help you solve. Since your stories have appeared in the *Bridge*, I've come to believe you are doing fine by yourself, but I'm curious to know what you think of our American school."

"I like it," she answered promptly. "But I think if I had walked in, for the first time, just now, I'd be scornful. I'd be thinking, 'Why are all these students wasting so much time and getting so excited over an election? Why aren't they studying instead?' "

"And now?"

"Now I think it's fine. We'll all be voting in a few years and it is important to learn how and why. Especially how to judge whom you are voting for." Katherine sat down on a straight-backed chair and put her books in her lap.

He nodded. "You're here to get an education. That comes first—books and classes. It's just as much a part of your education, however, to learn how to live in an adult world; how to work with others. We want to develop Katherine Norman as an individual; we also want to see Katherine Norman learn to work in a group."

She thought for a moment. "That's the way it is in the *Bridge* office. We all have our special jobs, but when you put them all together, it makes a newspaper. Sometimes, of course, we all have to pitch in and help each other and do each other's jobs, but most of the time we are separate individuals—"

"Working collectively. Right," he finished for her. "Now to business. Miss Sunderman tells me you have done extremely well and you are up to and past the juniors in your study of American history. She thinks it would be possible for you to take journalism next semester if you are willing to work privately with her. She's willing to give you the extra time; make up a course of study for you; and, if you will continue to hand in as good papers and reports as you've been doing, we will count that as completing a course for you. Are you willing to take on this work?"

"Miss Sunderman is nice," she blurted out. "Of course I will do it. I'd love to."

"Then that's settled," and he dismissed her with a smile.

Katherine had intended to go straight home after school and study hard; but there had been no chance for her to thank Miss Sunderman during the class, so she headed for the American history room. The door was slightly open as she passed the art room, not enough to see who was in the room but just enough to catch a glimpse of a figure bending over some posters. It crossed Katherine's mind that someone was working late; she was surprised because the posters were all supposed to have been finished and ready to put up the next morning. Whoever was in there closed the door quickly. She heard it shut as she walked past.

She dismissed it from her mind when she walked into Miss Sunderman's room.

"I want to thank you for all you've done for me, all the extra attention you've given me, Miss Sunderman," she said.

The teacher jabbed a pencil into her untidy hair. "Don't thank me. Wait until you see how I make you work next semester. Hah! You won't think I'm so kind. And right now I have some extra work for you. In addition to the exam the whole class will take next week, I expect from you an outline of the events leading up to the Civil War. By an outline I mean a listing of the main points and, underneath, the subheadings one, two, three, and so forth."

Katherine wasn't upset. She knew by now that Miss Sunderman never demanded more of her than she could do.

The teacher took a book from her desk. "This is the best source material, right here. I'll show you the pages to read. But you'll have to do it right here, right now. This is my one and only copy and I never lend it out. Unfortunately the library doesn't have it. It should take you about an hour or so."

Katherine took the book to her own desk. For a while she worked steadily, in silence, and so did Miss Sunderman. Occasionally the teacher would break the mood with a muttered "Oh, dear, I do hate grading papers," or a fierce "Now I told Bobby to watch how he spelled 'prairie fire' and 'buffalo'!" And once, after half an hour's silence, she burst out, "Honestly, Katherine, the best thing that happened to you in Europe is that you did learn how to spell. Our American students just don't know how."

It was quiet in the building. Once in a while there were voices in the hall outside. Sometimes a door slammed; but as the minutes went on, the school became more and more quiet and there were not even footsteps outside. Katherine's outline was running beyond the hour intended. It must be nearly five o'clock.

She raised her head suddenly. Miss Sunderman said, "What's that?" Both had heard the strangest sound . . . as if something had fallen or been dropped with a bang. The noise was outside the room but not far away. It was a thud and a crash, from next door, perhaps, or across the hall. They both listened; but when the sound was not repeated Miss Sunderman shrugged her shoulders and said, "Some student must have dropped a lot of books," and they both went back to work.

Finally Katherine was finished. She sighed, stretched her arms to ease her back muscles, took the book back to Miss Sunderman's desk. "Thank you for lending it to me," she said.

"Finished? Good. I'm almost done, myself. I'll see you tomorrow, Katherine." The teacher gathered her papers and stacked them neatly.

"Shall I wait for you, Miss Sunderman?"

"No, you run along. I have to tidy up for a second and turn out lights and lock the door."

Katherine walked slowly out into the hall, thinking about the examinations coming up. The one on English Lit, for Miss Mailer, would be the most difficult; she would have to do a lot of reviewing on that one. Miss Sunderman's wouldn't be hard, in spite of this extra work.

As she walked by the door of the art room she noticed, again, that it was slightly open. Something that Miss Sunderman said came to Katherine's mind: "I have to . . . turn out lights and lock the door." The lights in the art room were all on and the door was open. Was someone in there? She stopped. All down the hallways she noticed the doors were tightly shut. On a sudden impulse she glanced inside the art room to see if anyone really was there.

The room was empty. At first glance everything seemed fine. Katherine let her eye wander all around the room—and that was when she saw it, the gap, the broken line in the neat rows of posters stacked against the wall. It registered in her mind even before she knew what it meant. She had seen that room earlier. All around the wall, down by the floor, filling every inch of space, were the posters.

Now there was one large empty space. When she looked again, she saw that the posters which should have been standing in that area were flat on the floor—and they were a sight!

Horrified, she walked over and examined them. They were slashed and torn and ripped to pieces. At least twenty posters were now just bits of paper and sticks of wood. That must have been the strange sound she had heard. Whoever had done this had let some of them fall while the savage destruction had been going on.

She knelt down and turned over part of one poster. There was just the chin of a girl with the letters, underneath, "——rite" and "——elley."

Marguerite Kelley. Someone had torn up all of the posters with Marguerite's picture and name on them! Though she was not supposed to look at the candidates' posters, Katherine didn't care now: she went from one stack to another, searching. Not one of Marguerite's posters was left standing; not a single one of the other candidate's had even been disturbed.

The horror of such maliciousness, such cruelty, shocked Katherine. Who could have done it?

"Who could have done it?"

The words in her mind had been spoken out loud, by somebody else, and she wheeled to see Miss Sunderman, who must have come quietly into the room, staring at the havoc on the floor. "Who could have done it?" she repeated. "In my years as a teacher I've seen some nasty things, but this is one of the worst. Just wanton destruction, to hurt a very, very nice girl like Marguerite Kelley; so that tomorrow when the posters go up she won't have them and her opponent will. Who is the other candidate? I don't remember."

"Jet Smith," Katherine answered her, sinking into a chair. Looking up at Miss Sunderman, she was quick to see a look of distaste and disgust on her face.

There were heavy footsteps outside in the hall. Miss Sunderman darted out and came back, bringing Mr. Johns with her. He studied the havoc on the floor and listened quietly as Miss Sunderman related the events leading up to the discovery. Katherine had seen Mr. Johns when he was serious, when he was gay; now his anger sent a shiver up her spine.

"Did either of you hear or see anything else suspicious?" he asked.

Katherine remembered, then, the partly open door she had

passed earlier and the figure she had glimpsed inside the room.

"You didn't recognize him—or her? You couldn't be sure whether it was a boy or a girl? Or whether there was only one person or more?"

Katherine shook her head. "No, I can't be sure. I just glanced in and I didn't recognize the figure. It was just a quick impression. Then I heard a noise later on. What can be done about this, Mr. Johns? It's so important to Marguerite. She's so quiet and you hardly know she's around; so people are apt to forget about her. If there are no posters tomorrow, calling attention to her, and all those posters of Jet—I'm afraid she'll lose." She twisted in her chair, but she couldn't bear to look at the torn-up posters.

"What can be done? Nothing. Not right now. I'll have to ask you not to say a word about this, except to certain very trusted people. Bob Macdonald will have to know. If you see him, tell him to come to my office the first thing tomorrow morning so that I can tell him what to print in the paper. This will have to be called an accident, Katherine. It *is* an accident—but a beastly one, done on purpose."

"I don't understand. Why shouldn't I tell?"

He walked away from her and stood at the window, looking out. His voice reflected his unhappy mood. "Because I've had experience with similar things. You'd like me to announce at a special assembly that some unknown person or persons crept into this room after school and willfully, wickedly destroyed Marguerite's posters. It would gain sympathy for her; but if I did that, the results would be nothing short of disastrous to the school and to the senior class. Examinations are coming up next week, and for the seniors these are important; their grades will determine whether they get into college or not."

He turned back from the window and faced her, standing very straight and tall and commanding. "I've seen before what could happen, Katherine. All kinds of wild rumors and gossip flying around; students trying to play detective; students suspecting

170

each other; someone mentioning a name and everyone condemning that person without a hearing. Innocent people getting their names smeared. Quarrels breaking out. Accusations flying back and forth. The classrooms seething with ugly talk, suspicion, a bad kind of excitement. No one can study in such an atmosphere. The entire senior class—and some of the rest of the school—will suffer from poor grades."

"But, Mr. Johns, Marguerite can lose the election. She's sure to!" Katherine could see the truth of what he said; still, it seemed unjust.

"I know. The tragedy will all fall on her. She's the one who will suffer, but Marguerite is a very sensible person and she'd be the first to say that I'm right. After all, she has held office before; it will hurt her, but it won't break her heart if she loses this one. I know Marguerite."

He looked at his watch. "Getting late, Katherine. It's time you were getting home. And I have work to do. I have to call the principal and other teachers and arrange a conference on this for tomorrow morning. You have my promise that we won't let this thing go unpunished. We'll handle it very quietly, but it's been my experience that sooner or later we find the guilty party. We have ways of finding these things out. You run along and leave it to us—and, Katherine"—as she moved slowly toward the door—"do I have your promise? To everyone but Bob you will say only that you heard there had been an accident to the posters? Nothing more? Good girl."

Miss Sunderman had been standing, arms akimbo, one foot angrily tapping the floor, even though she had nodded her head in agreement with what Mr. Johns had said. Now she burst out, as Katherine was leaving, "It's a rotten shame! Marguerite's such a nice girl. I do think, Mr. Johns, that it would be all right for Katherine to talk to her. I know Katherine's just bursting with this and I'm sure Marguerite will want to talk to somebody, if only for consolation. We'll phone her first, from your office, but it's too much to expect the two girls not to want to discuss this together."

With this much granted her, Katherine had to be satisfied, even though everything in her cried out against the injustice. Sick with anger, facing her first real tragedy, Katherine went home.

12

"Whoever did it," she exploded to Aunt Debra when she reached home, "is going to get away with it. Even if he or she gets caught, eventually, the scheme was to win the election for Jet and that's just what will happen."

Aunt Debra flapped her apron at her. "Calm down. I can't make heads or tails of what you're saying. Go ahead and call Bob and Marguerite, if you want to, and I'll listen. But tell it step by step so I'll understand."

She phoned. Marguerite already knew and was trying to take it calmly, but Katherine caught the quiver of tears in her voice. "I know. Mr. Johns told me. We'll just have to do what he says, Katherine. I didn't think anyone hated me like that." The quiver became a sob.

"I don't think anyone hates you," Katherine protested. "Someone thought it was a clever trick to win an election, that's all." She had a sudden inspiration, knowing how awful it is to be alone when you are miserable. "Why don't you come over here, Marguerite. Have dinner with Aunt Debra and me?"

"I'll be right over," the other agreed quickly. "If we talk it out tonight it won't be so hard not to say anything tomorrow."

Bob didn't even let her finish the story. "I'll be right over. I want to hear *this* straight."

Aunt Debra had been listening. "One guest for dinner? If I know Bob Macdonald, we'll have two. He'll stay. You go into that kitchen and put some of your fanciest touches on the dinner. I'll make a fire in the fireplace and then I have to go out for a while."

"Out? Now?" Katherine was surprised.

"Yes. I have to go back to Landero's. It's something I forgot to do—to get—in the office. Don't wait dinner for me; the three of you go ahead and eat."

When she was left alone and rushing around the kitchen, Katherine had to face the question that had been burning in her own mind. Who? Who had done this thing? Jet? It didn't seem possible and yet it was probable. He was capable of reckless, stupid things; so many times had he come to the border line of actually doing something very wrong, it was easy to suspect him. Had he stepped over that border this time?

I won't say anything, she resolved, when she heard the door-bell ring. I would be doing just what Mr. Johns said: making an accusation when I don't know for sure, and perhaps Jet is innocent.

Both Bob and Marguerite, she saw, were equally careful not to mention his name or anyone else's as they sat her down before the fire and made her tell them exactly what she had seen and heard in the art room and what had happened to the posters. They talked of everything else except— Who?

They ate their dinner on trays in front of the fire but none of them had any appetite. "It's the dirtiest trick I've ever heard," said Bob. "What kind of mind or minds would think of such a thing? It would take somebody childish as well as mean."

"Childish or not, it's lost the election for me. I wouldn't care so much if Jet Smith would be a good vice-president; but I think he'll just give it a whirl for a couple of weeks next term and then get bored with it, and the other officers will have to do all the work." It was unusual for Marguerite to be so bitter.

"We can't be sure you'll lose," protested Katherine.

"I'm sure." Marguerite was honest about herself. "I didn't put on any razzle-dazzle campaign as he did; and when there aren't any posters of me around tomorrow, that will just tip the balance. There are a lot of students who don't know either of us very well; they'll see his name and his face and his platform on those posters and, when they go to vote, that's what they'll remember."

Bob put down his tray, his food only half eaten, and got up to pace the floor. "I'd like to hit somebody! If there were only something we could do—"

Katherine heard the key in the door but it seemed to be taking Aunt Debra quite some time to come in. They could hear bumpings and she was walking slowly, as if burdened down. "Come here and help me!" she called. "I can't carry all these things, myself."

"What things?" Katherine went out into the hall. "Why, Aunt Debra—what on earth? What do you have there?"

"Posters. At least they are the making of posters. When you said posters, I remembered all that white pasteboard in the advertising office. Landero makes thousands of cards and posters for display purposes all over the store. So I asked the advertising chief—I knew he would still be there, working on January sales layouts—and he said, certainly, take all I wanted, in such a good cause. He said he had a son in high school, too. And he gave me inks of all colors, and pencils."

They stared at her and she stared back at them, belligerently. "Well," she said, "you aren't going to take this lying down, are you? You aren't going to let those villains get away with it? We're going to have posters tomorrow."

"Aunt Debra!" yelled Bob.

"Aunt Debra!" echoed Katherine.

Only Marguerite objected. "We can't do much in one night. It's taken an artist and five helpers all week to make up enough posters to compete with the others."

"Hmmph. We can do what we can," said Aunt Debra, letting pasteboards and packages fall and scatter all over tables and floor. "Come on. Put lots of newspapers on the dining-room table and we'll all work from there. They won't be good posters and they won't be clever ones; but we'll see that your name is on them, anyway."

Full of excitement so heady that she wanted to shout or do what Bob was doing—pound Aunt Debra on the back—Katherine gathered up the materials. They were spread out on the table on top of newspapers. Aunt Debra had brought crayons and colored inks in yellow, blue, red, greens and blacks; pens and pencils. The older woman placed a stack of poster material in front of her and gave orders: "We'll do this on an assembly-line basis. I can make clear, even letters in print. Can anyone else? Bob? All right, you and I will do the original lettering, very lightly, in pencil. Then the girls can fill in, with the colored inks."

Bob sat down next to her and pulled a white rectangular poster board toward him. "There's no use doing anything too ambitious. I think we just write MARGUERITE KELLEY in great, big letters and underneath that 'For Senior Class Vice-President.' Then on some, in small type, we can write 'For your own best interests, vote for Marguerite.' "

"All right. I'll do that one." Aunt Debra began to make bold, clear strokes with her pencil, using a ruler to make the letters even.

"Another one"—Katherine had nothing to do yet, so she was busy dividing up the colored inks and crayons between herself and Marguerite—"could say A VOTE FOR MARGUERITE KELLEY IS A VOTE FOR GOOD GOVERNMENT, or something like that." She was so happy she was laughing as she spoke. Even Marguerite's usually sober face was bright.

Bob was grinning, too. He put his pencil down, saying he had an idea. "I'm going to call Penlon, the guy who draws the cartoons for the *Bridge*, and see if he can come over and help us." But the fat artist was not at home, nor did his mother expect him until late. "It was a good try anyway," Bob said as he slid back into his chair. "I guess we'd better not waste time trying to phone anyone else. We're going to have to work hard to get even a few done."

As fast as Aunt Debra or Bob finished with one faintly lettered poster, Katherine or Marguerite grabbed it and began the careful, slow, tedious job of filling in the letters. Neither was an artist and, at best, the finished posters were dull and uninspired; the worst ones looked like something a child had botched up. But there would be posters tomorrow!

The doorbell rang. "Will you get it, Bob?" Katherine asked. "I've got green ink all over my fingers and if I leave this letter it will get dry and not match the others."

From the dining room they could hear him at the door saying, "Hi, Troy. No, you can't come in. Big secret."

"I don't want to come in; I want you to come home. Did you forget that tonight's the night our family trims our Christmas tree? We're all waiting for you and, believe me, our little brother is about to bawl his head off."

"I can't come. I'll call Mom and explain to her, but it's none of your business. You go ahead without me."

"What's going on?" she protested. "You can't fool me. What is it I'm not supposed to know?"

Katherine heard him cry out "Hey, come back here!" but Troy was already in the living room staring at what they were doing, through the dining-room arch. "Why, that's illegal. You're making more posters for Marguerite and you aren't supposed to. We all finished tonight; we all were allowed exactly the same number, every candidate. Nobody is supposed to have more than the others and I know that Marguerite's were finished because Penlon told me so." She was so indignant that for a second she didn't see Aunt Debra. When she recognized the older woman she apologized, but she was still angry. "I'm sorry, Aunt Debra. I didn't mean to yell at you."

"We aren't doing more posters." Bob came up behind her and said, "There was an accident and Marguerite's posters were all ruined."

Troy swung around to look at him. "What do you mean—an accident? Don't try to kid me, Bob. We're twins, remember. I know every tone of your voice and just what it means. I can read your mind. What kind of accident? Why were Marguerite's—" A thought struck her and she looked panicky. "What about Jet's? Were his ruined, too?"

What had been just a tiny fear, one that Katherine had pushed down inside her and refused to acknowledge, melted away. There had been seconds when she had wondered if the whole Crowd had been behind the destruction, and if the whole Crowd also meant Troy. But Troy's astonishment and her fears were too genuine. She knew nothing about this.

"No," Bob was saying as he resumed his place at the table, "Jet's are all right. Everyone's are all right—except Marguerite's."

Troy was left standing alone. She looked at the four bent heads, four pairs of hands working at the table, and there was suspicion on her face. She took a step forward, uncertainly, and then another one. "Something's going on here and I think there's been dirty work. You might as well tell me; I'll find out. How did this 'accident' happen?"

Katherine put down her pen and wiped her hands on a rag already stained all colors. "We'd better tell her, Bob, even if I did promise Mr. Johns. I know that Troy won't tell anyone, not even Chap, if she promises she won't."

"Not if she gives *me* her word," said Aunt Debra grimly. "She never lied to me when she was a kid and she won't now. You're working for another candidate; so, in a sense, that makes you an enemy in our camp, Troy, but I trust you. Go on, Katherine."

So once more Katherine had to tell the story.

Troy listened intently. "I know who did it," she said promptly.

"Who?" asked Bob and Katherine together.

"Jet?" asked Marguerite.

Troy shook her head. "No, not Jet. He wouldn't be so stupid. It might win him an election, but it would be bound to come

178

out, sometime, and do him a lot of harm. No, I know; but I'm not saying. I have no proof." She turned to face Katherine, so that no one else could see her, and her lips framed the name George Yale.

Of course. Immediately Katherine knew it was true. It could be only George Yale—so pathetically anxious to win the election for his hero, Jet; so willing to do anything he thought would win him a pat on the back from Jet. George Yale, who always managed to say and do the wrong thing, would be exactly the one to think he had done a clever thing. He must be home now, gloating over his action and anticipating that this time the Crowd would applaud him, make him belong.

The phone rang.

"My, this is a busy house this evening," complained Aunt Debra, not stopping work for a moment.

"It must be Mom. I'll go smooth her feathers down." Troy went out into the hall and they could hear her saying, "No, Mom, we can't come. It's an emergency. Honest. A *real* emergency. I'll tell you all about it when we come home. I know— I can hear him! Tell him it's like that TV program—the bad guy has done something awful and so Bob and I are the good guys who are putting it right. Tell little brother I'll give him one of his Christmas presents tomorrow. It's a chemistry set and he can blow us all up. That will make him happy."

She came back, taking off her coat.

"Did I hear you say 'we'?" Bob asked.

"Don't give me any trouble," his sister commanded. "You just got demoted. You move over there with the girls and get your fingers all full of paint. Aunt Debra and I are going to draw these posters. I'm not doing this out of the goodness of my heart," she joked, "but my artistic sense won't let you put out those poor, pathetic posters tomorrow." She took up a pencil and squinted along its edge at Marguerite. "Ah! Got it! I'll do a profile on you and a cartoon sketch that will knock 'em dead."

"Troy," whispered Katherine gratefully, happily, joyfully. And Aunt Debra took a second out to reach over and pat the girl's hand. "You're a nice child, Troy Macdonald. I always thought so."

Not only did Troy's fingers fairly fly over the heavy white sheets, but she kept up a running fire of comments that had them all laughing. "You'll be the glamour-girl candidate when I get through with this sketch, Marguerite. You'll have all the guys howling like wolves. But don't you think we should get some snap in these posters? How about MARK YOUR BALLOT FOR MARGUERITE? OR MARCH FORWARD WITH MARGUERITE? OR KEEP UP WITH KELLEY? I like that. Or how about some verse? Onwards, senior class; upwards, with this lass—*Kelly*!" She gave a flourish with her pencil.

Bob grinned. "We'll do that one. I'm serious. It's good. And how about one of those with K-E-L-L-E-Y, running down the left-hand side, and opposite the K—Knowledge. Opposite the E—Enterprise. Opposite the one L—Leadership. Opposite the other L—"

"Liverwurst," suggested Marguerite. Troy half rose in her chair, leaned over and tapped Marguerite on the head with her pencil. "That for you! Cutie-pie, you *do* have a sense of humor after all."

"Stop all this fooling around." Aunt Debra tried to be stern. "I can do that poster; it doesn't require any drawing. Think up another L—something for me."

They tossed ideas back and forth, while their hands were busy with the work. Troy talked a lot and chattered, but that didn't affect the swiftness of her drawing. She handed Marguerite the first one she finished and Katherine the second. "Make the hair dark but go easy on the other colors. Too much red on the lips will make it look ridiculous."

Her third drawing was a masterpiece and they all agreed it should have no color at all, just light and dark strokes of the pencil. Somehow, in spite of Troy's trivial nonsense, she had sensitively caught the very essence of Marguerite's character in that drawing—the chin was fluent but pure of line; the eyes looked straightforward, honest and true. The mouth was just faintly, faintly smiling.

"A cross between Joan of Arc and Florence Nightingale," Troy said, but there was kindness behind her flippancy and Katherine loved her for it. It seemed so good to have Troy here again; and so specially good to see brother and sister working together, teasing each other, bickering sometimes but not quarreling. The twinship between Bob and Troy had never been so apparent before.

"Do a funny one next, Troy," Bob ordered her. "I have an idea. A lot of figures in the background—students—all of them looking in different directions, up, down, sideways. And underneath it we'll print 'WHICH WAY?—FOLLOW KELLEY.' How's that?"

"It's an awful idea, but I'll do it." And it turned out not to be awful at all, but very eye-catching.

They worked steadily and hard for two hours, then Katherine said, "We'll break in ten minutes and give our muscles a chance to stretch. I'll go in and get us something to eat."

"Ah, food. I'm starved. We were too upset to eat much dinner," Bob said.

"Well, I haven't had any dinner at all." This from Aunt Debra.

"Aunt Debra! Of course you haven't. You went to the store and came right back and started to work. I never realized until just this moment—" Katherine was dismayed. Her aunt gave her a chiding look which said *Don't disturb our guests and make them feel uncomfortable,* and Katherine smiled back at her. They were family; they were Normans; they understood each other.

While she arranged cake and plates on the tray and waited

for Aunt Debra's coffee to perk, Troy wandered out to the kitchen. "Need any help?" she asked, breaking off a small piece of cake and nibbling on it.

"No—but, Troy," lowering her voice, "I've been wondering. Won't the Crowd be angry when they hear you worked for Marguerite as well as for Jet?"

Troy shrugged. "The Crowd is practically no more. It's breaking up. You started it, or maybe George Yale coming in started it; I don't know. But the finishing touch was this campaign of Jet's. We got into something big, something real. Chap and I found out we liked spending time talking to the other kids and we began to make new friends. We're still going steady with each other; but we don't want to go round and round in circles with the same small bunch, seeing the same old faces and doing the same old things."

"I'm so glad." Katherine could have hugged her. "I was just dreading Christmas coming and not being able to see you and talk to you and spend some of the holidays with you."

"Then you'd better buy me a present," grinned Troy. "I have yours all wrapped up and put away in the closet."

They worked steadily until eleven o'clock and then Aunt Debra called a halt. "It's late now and tomorrow is school for you and the job for me. Let's see—we have twelve really good ones and three others that aren't too bad. Will that do, Marguerite?"

"It's a lifesaver, Miss Norman. I just can't thank you enough for what you've done for me. I was trying to pretend I didn't care, but I just felt like crying until you walked in with all those packages."

Bob kissed Aunt Debra and so did Troy. Katherine walked to the door to say good-by to their guests. Bob had the posters safe under his arm, except for two still drying in the dining room. Katherine put her arm around her aunt's waist and hugged her tight. Closing the door, she said, "You are absolutely wonderful, Aunt Debra. I was so proud of you tonight. I'm so glad I came to live with you."

"I'm—" Aunt Debra was having difficulty with her throat. She cleared it, twice. She spoke sternly, as if she were afraid of sentiment. "You get to bed, quick. That dining room's a mess and it will just have to be a mess. I'm not going to do one more lick of work. I never left a room that untidy," she grumbled, climbing the stairs after her niece, "until you came. Never!"

The next day the whole school was alive with posters. Every time Katherine passed one of Marguerite's she found herself breaking out into a smile. Mr. Johns had been astonished and pleased when he heard what they had done. "Now there won't even be so many questions or rumors around. If the students who worked on the old posters ask what happened to them, we'll say it was an accident; and if they are persistent, send them in to me and I'll answer their questions."

Katherine didn't mention George Yale. She had no proof. She had perfect faith that Mr. Johns would, in his own way and his own time, uncover the culprit and administer the right punishment.

Friday afternoon she was in the *Bridge* office the minute her last class was ended. She walked in just as Bob was holding up a copy of the *Bridge* still wet with printer's ink, fresh off the press. The headlines read: "SENIOR CLASS ELECTIONS: PRESIDENT: MANUEL PERADA. VICE-PRESIDENT: MARGUERITE KELLEY."

Katherine didn't read any further. The rest of the staff was jubilant over winning candidates, sad at their losses; the office was pandemonium. She looked across as Audrey's head bobbed in excitement as she called out the new officers, and smiled at Bob. He winked back. He came over to her desk and whispered, "She made it!"

"Do you think the posters had something to do with it?" Katherine whispered back.

"I think so. She won by a very small margin. It was a close race."

"I'm glad. Jet will have a setback and that will be good for him, but the close race will save his pride."

Bob frowned. "Why do you care what happens to him?"

"I don't know why, but I do," Katherine replied. "He's not bad; he's just reckless and thoughtless. Maybe this will teach him he has to work for recognition."

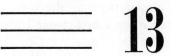

13

The next week was hectic for Katherine. It was exams and studying for exams; flying downtown to the stores for Christmas shopping; collecting lumpy packages from Mr. Bean from Italy —with her name and Aunt Debra's in Daddy's familiar handwriting. She felt a sudden twinge of homesickness for Daddy and all the Christmases they had shared.

"Except in the big cities, where they've borrowed the custom from other countries, Italians don't go in for Christmas trees," she told Bob one evening as they stood in the circle of the bay window. Across the street she could see the shining splendor of the lighted tree in the Macdonald house. "So Daddy used to say, 'Wait until you're in America; then you'll see a real Christmas, with the tree and lights and decorations.' I've argued and argued, but Aunt Debra still says no."

Now that the ice was broken, Bob and Troy wandered in and out of the Norman house. Aunt Debra might scold and say she never had a moment's peace any more; but Katherine suspected that her aunt liked having company and didn't even mind the noise, the laughter and the banging of doors.

"She's set in her ways; that's what my Dad says," agreed Bob. He pulled gently at one of Katherine's short red curls. Since the night he had tried to kiss her and she had been shy of him, he had kept a little distance between them. Just the same, when he touched her like this, she could feel her own heart pounding and she wondered what he was feeling. "She doesn't like changes," he said.

With difficulty Katherine brought her thoughts back to Aunt Debra.

"Sometimes I think she's changed a lot," she said slowly, "and then something happens and she's almost the way she was at first. Do you know I almost hated her when I first came? I was a little scared of her."

"I'll bet she was a little scared of you, too. After all, she lived so quietly and then to have a beautiful young girl, with a stubborn chin and full of energy, land suddenly on her—all she could do was roll herself up in a ball like a porcupine, stick her quills out and pretend you weren't there."

When he left, she went to her mirror. He had called her "beautiful." She studied herself and turned away, disappointed. She wasn't the least bit beautiful. Her chin *was* stubborn.

Bob thinks I'm beautiful. That's what matters. He must think so or he wouldn't have said it, and I only want to be beautiful for him. Katherine was stunned to realize how very much she wanted it and how much it mattered to her what Bob Macdonald thought of her. Her heart was pounding again. This feeling was so new she didn't know what to make of it.

Friday came and that afternoon she walked home with the weight of the exams off her shoulders. She knew she had passed; in fact, she knew she had done well. She felt free and exhilarated. The holidays stretched ahead of her with no work, no studying; with days and days in which to do just as she pleased.

Coming into the house was a shock. She had become so accustomed to the house and for the past week had been so busy studying that she hadn't realized until that moment how quiet, how dismal, how un-Christmasy it was. Aunt Debra had strung one small loop of lights across the bay window—that was all. A few wrapped packages, some from Daddy, sat forlornly on the small table near the sofa.

I won't have it, she thought to herself. I just won't!

She counted the money in her purse and it was exactly four dollars and twenty cents, all that was left over from the Christmas money her father had sent her; all that was left over after she had bought a silk scarf for Aunt Debra, a dance record for Troy, a pen for Bob and a book she had sent to Daddy.

It wasn't much but it would do. She flew out of the house and down to the stores on the next corner. An hour later she was back and loaded down with packages. The great spray of poinsettias went into the blue mosaic vase she brought down from her bedroom; over the fireplace mantel they made a vivid, elegant glory of red and blue.

She found, on the top shelf of one of the kitchen cabinets, a silver candelabra with four branching candlesticks. It was tarnished and she had to rub hard with silver polish before it shone. Then she put the four tall red candles she had bought in it. That was for the table, to gleam over the Christmas packages.

Into a cut-glass bowl she piled blue and gold and silver balls, the kind she ached so much to hang on a tree, but this would have to do. Set on the dining-room table, it brightened up the whole room. On the living-room coffee table she constructed a winter snow scene, with a two-foot mirror for a skating rink and cotton piled around the edges for snow. Toy trees and a toy house nestled among the cotton, and little red and white skating figures made of pipe cleaners were skating, falling, dancing all over the mirror.

Then she went into the kitchen. A fruit cake was too ambitious for her, she decided. But she remembered a Danish friend of her father's who had taught her how to bake the special caraway ring cake which the Danes ate for Christmas breakfast. It was delicious and had a cinnamon glaze to the top of it.

There was a phone call from Aunt Debra. "I'll be home a little late this evening. The advertising department is in a jam and they insist I'm the only secretary they can depend on, to help them out of it." She didn't sound as if she resented the extra work; in fact, she sounded very self-satisfied. "I'll have dinner here at the store cafeteria."

Another phone call. "Is Miss Norman there? No? That's too

bad. This is Mr. Dale from the Marlborough. Would you ask her to call me here at the hotel, no matter how late she comes in? It's important."

It sounded important. Katherine wondered what it could be.

When the phone rang again she was ready to snap with exasperation, but it was Bob and she relaxed. "Can I come over this evening? Later? Exams are finished and we have to celebrate!"

"Fine. Do come," she urged. "But I have to run; I have something in the oven and it's going to burn, any minute."

When Aunt Debra walked in, at eight o'clock, she saw the poinsettias first and said, "Well!" Next she saw the candles lit above their silver stems and said "Well!" again. She sniffed the air. "Something certainly smells good. What have you been up to?" Then she looked at the snow scene on the coffee table.

"Do you mind, Aunt Debra? It doesn't make any muss. I'll clean it up after Christmas."

Aunt Debra touched one of the skating figures and it toppled over. She carefully put it back on its wobbly legs. "No, I don't mind, child." Her voice was subdued and puzzled and thoughtful. Her eyes traveled over the living room and into the dining room, catching the tumbled splash of colors in the cut-glass bowl. "I hardly know the house. It's so different. It's so *gay*."

Katherine remembered. "Oh, you have an important telephone call from Mr. Dale. He wants you to call the Marlborough immediately. He says it's very urgent and important."

Without even taking off her coat, and walking as if in a daze, Aunt Debra went to the phone in the hall. It was a long conversation and it seemed to Katherine that Mr. Dale was doing most of the talking. All Aunt Debra said were things like "Is that so?" and "I'm not a bit surprised" and "Well, now—I just don't know. I'll have to think it over, Mr. Dale. Thank you, just the same."

When it was over and she came back into the living room, she did not sit down. She stood looking into the fire and once she poked at a log, with her foot.

"Well? Is it something really important, Aunt Debra?"

The older woman started, as if coming out of deep thought. "Oh, yes. They want me to come back. They're in a mess at the hotel; the secretary they hired isn't working out at all. They want me to come back to my old job, with a raise in pay and full responsibility."

"That's wonderful. I know how happy you are about it," Katherine exclaimed. "I know how much you've missed it."

"I'm not happy about it," snapped Aunt Debra with a return of her usual manner. "It's a nice boost to my pride, but I don't want to go back there. Twenty years at one job is just too long; I was in a rut. Every day the same thing, the same work—no, it hurt when I had to leave, but it was the very best thing that could have happened. It shook me out of my habits and I found out I liked the challenge of learning something new. I'm still considered a temporary at Landero's, but I'm going to gamble that they'll keep me on. I feel it in my bones that the advertising department wants me and that's what I want. I'm not going to go back," she said fiercely, "to the same old business of smoothing down temperamental head waiters and worrying over how many pillowcases the housekeeper needs. I like this advertising business!" She glared at Katherine as if it were she who was defying her.

"You don't *mind* changes? Then, Aunt Debra, you don't really mind my being here and living with you?"

"Mind?" Aunt Debra looked at her and suddenly her whole face seemed to crumple and change and soften. Her lips quivered. "Katherine—I—"

The doorbell saved her. Katherine saw her get a grip on herself and straighten up, and she smiled to herself with a new and affectionate understanding of her aunt. The older woman had been about to say something tender and loving; it was too hard for her to say it and Katherine didn't care if the words were ever spoken. At that moment she knew Aunt Debra really loved her very much.

"It's Bob," she said softly. "I'll go."

She didn't know quite why it was that she didn't let Bob into the house right away; instead she went out on the porch beside him. "Isn't it a lovely night?" she said, looking up at the clear, dark sky dotted with stars. The air was fresh and cool and all along the streets the Christmas decorations were a radiant procession of color and lights. Above it all, above the city, she could just see the gleaming illumination of the spires of the Golden Gate Bridge.

"Yes, it's lovely," he said. "And so are you."

It was so easy, then, and she didn't feel shy. She took one step toward him and he took one toward her and she was in his arms. He kissed her and then for a long moment they stood like that, with her cheek against his, and inside her there was both a quiet joyfulness and a crazy happiness.

"We'd better go in," she said, at last, whispering it.

"Yes. We'd better."

They found Aunt Debra comfortably sitting in the big chair in front of the fire, a plate of the freshly baked caraway cake on her lap. She was looking around the room with a disdainful air. "It looks pretty, Katherine. You've fixed it up nicely. But what it needs," she said with a determined nod, as if no one had ever mentioned it before and it was entirely her own idea, "is a Christmas tree in that bay window!"